LET ME LOVE YOU

Winter Lake

RHIAN CAHILL

Rhian Cahill

Let Me Love You
Winter Lake
By Rhian Cahill

Love Me Like You Do
Love The Way You Are
When You Love Someone
Let Me Love You
Wild Rush Of Love

LET ME LOVE YOU
WINTER LAKE BOOK 4

He's got moves on — and off — the field.

As receiver for the Miami Storm, Grady Murdock couldn't be more satisfied with his professional life. Next up—his personal one. He's a player on the field, not off, so when he claps eyes on Melinda at a Storm event, he's neither surprised nor alarmed to find she triggers both lustful and long-term thoughts. Six years his senior, Mel isn't so easily convinced.

Independent, career-minded Melinda Shaw has singlehandedly built one of Miami's premier event-management companies, but success hasn't stopped her heart from shifting its focus to marriage and children. Still, she's not about to burden a younger man with her fantasies of familial grandeur...until she does.

Their combustible sexual chemistry notwithstanding, Grady still has to work overtime to convince Mel he wants her despite their impending parenthood, not because of it. It'll take almost losing everything—and more than a few of Grady's famous moves—to score Mel's heart once and for all.

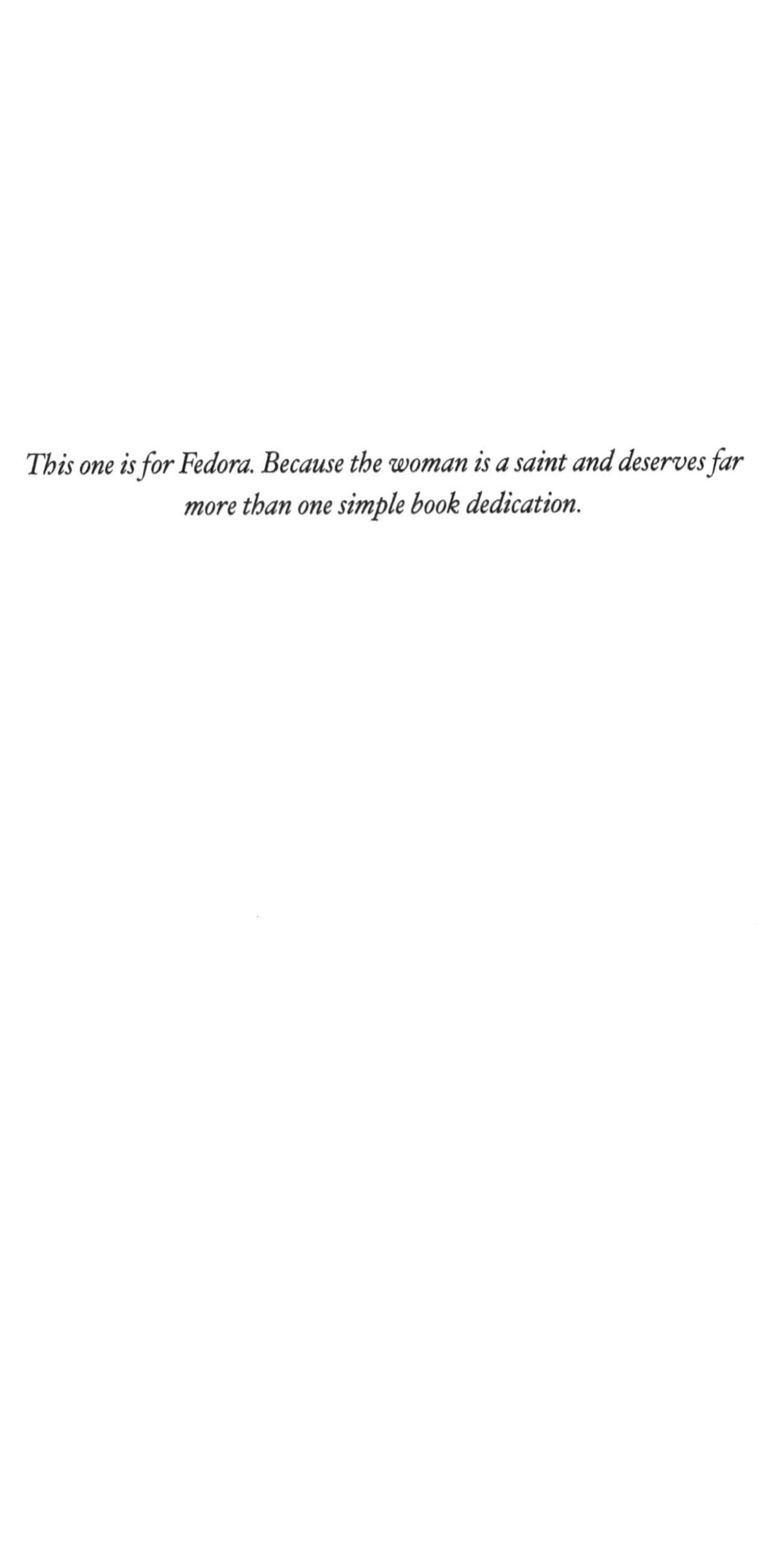

This one is for Fedora. Because the woman is a saint and deserves far more than one simple book dedication.

PROLOGUE
WINTER LAKE, NEW YORK

NOSE TINGLING, throat constricting, and eyes filling with tears, Mel stared at the vision in front of her. "Oh, Sadie."

Her best friend's smile wobbled and her eyes welled and widened. Waving a hand in front of her face, she implored, "Don't start. I can't mess up this makeup. It'll take too long to fix and I want to get this show on the road."

Mel sniffled and smiled through her tears. "I'm trying, but Sadie, you look so fucking gorgeous. Alex is going to swallow his tongue when he sees you."

"He better not. I've got plans for that tongue later," Sadie said with a laugh and a wink.

Laughing, Mel dabbed a tissue beneath her eyes to collect any moisture that may have leaked out and tried not to disturb her own makeup. "Speaking of shows..." She drew in a deep breath. "Are you ready?"

Smiling the most joyous smile Mel had ever seen on her best friend's face, Sadie said, "I was ready the second he asked me."

"I have to admit I'm surprised you two haven't snuck off to do the deed before now."

Sadie shrugged. "We thought about it, believe me, but I wanted to take our time with this. Everything else happened so fast. I wanted us to enjoy every step to this point."

"It wasn't that fast," Mel argued. "You've known each other since college."

"Yes, but we didn't really *know* know each other."

"True." Mel nodded. "But you know this is right, right?"

She wanted nothing but happiness for Sadie, except she and Alex had only reconnected a year ago—to the day—and while it was obvious to all they were deeply in love, Mel couldn't help the little bit of uncertainty that niggled at her.

"Mel, how long have you known me? How many times have I stumbled over making decisions?"

"Lots of times." Which was the problem.

Sadie had always been a little awkward in social situations and Mel could count the number of friendships Sadie had had over the years on one hand.

Although she had to admit over the last year Sadie had come out of her shell. She'd found Alex, moved to a new town, started a new job, which all came with new friends. She'd blossomed into the woman Mel had always known she could be if she would just believe in herself.

And when Mel thought about all those stumbles in the past she saw a pattern. The stumbles were over little things. Things that didn't matter.

The big choices—leaving Miami for a quieter life in a small town, quitting a high pressure job for one that had her excited to go to work every day...

Mel blew out a breath. "Yeah, okay, you know."

Sadie grinned. "I think I knew the day the soap arrived. It just took me a while to accept it."

"The soap?" Mel frowned. "Oh! The soap!" She laughed.

A tap on the door and a shouted, "You ladies ready?" had them both sucking in a breath.

"Ready?" Mel let her gaze travel the length of Sadie. From head to toe and back. Smiling, she said, "Yeah, we're ready."

"Before we go out there." Sadie stepped closer and grabbed both of Mel's hands in hers. "I know this is clichéd and you'll probably roll your eyes, but..." She squeezed Mel's hands. "I want this for you. The love, the joy, the partner who will do anything for you."

Sadie was right. Mel did roll her eyes. "I don't need that. Yet. I've got my ten-year plan and I'm only a few years in. There's time for me to find my 'Alex'." She pulled Sadie in for a hug, tried not to mess up makeup or hair or dresses.

"I love you," Sadie murmured.

"Love you too." Mel let go. "Now let's go make an honest man out of Alex."

Opening the door of the change room they'd taken over in Winter Lake Wears, Mel came face to face with one of those new friends Sadie had found in the past year.

"Is she ready?" Carly asked, her gaze excited but hesitant.

Mel understood the look; Sadie had really stepped out of her shell when it came to the wedding dress. "See for yourself," she said, stepping aside to let Sadie come out from behind her.

"Wow." Carly smiled. "You know I was worried when you told me what you were going to wear but holy shit, Alex is going to choke on his own tongue."

"Oh, sweetheart." Sadie's mom moved forward. "You look beautiful. I take back every word I said about an outside wedding and a non-traditional dress. The gazebo looks spectacular and that dress..." Mrs. Emerson choked up, shook her head, and wiped a tear from the corner of her eye.

Mel couldn't agree more. When Sadie had asked her to plan the wedding and they had talked about what she wanted, Mel had been a bit skeptical herself.

Hell, she'd been afraid the whole thing would be a disaster.

But now that it was done, now that Winter Lake Park and gazebo were dressed up to look like a winter fairy garden with twinkling lights and bubble blowing machines, she had to admit Sadie's vision was beyond beautiful.

It was magical.

And Sadie's dress? Its blue and green and brown tones was anything but traditional and something no one would ever imagine Sadie would wear.

The bodice, which dipped between her breasts to reveal a discreet amount of cleavage, hugged her torso to her hips before flowing out in waves of subtle color that swirled around her legs as she walked, making it appear as though she floated on air instead of walked on the ground.

Straps left her shoulders bare as they curved over her body and down her back where they crossed and rejoined the dress at her hips. Those inch-wide strips of material were what made up the back of the dress; nothing else covered her skin from neck to butt. With her long blonde hair in gentle ringlets, it wasn't obvious until Sadie moved that the dress was essentially backless.

Sadie looked like a magical woodland nymph.

Sexy and whimsical and otherworldly.

Mel had to choke back another wave of tears. This sensual creature was her socially awkward wallflower friend. The one she'd had to goad into saying hello to Alex the night they'd reconnected. The transformation was huge. Either the mountain air or Alex's love had triggered this metamorphosis.

Whatever the cause, Mel was thrilled by the changes in

her best friend. And a little sad. She hadn't been around for any of it. They'd been together for so long that the past year apart had been hard. But worth it.

Sadie had found the place she was meant to be here in Winter Lake—with Alex—and Mel had established her company as one of the top five event management firms in Miami.

Last year had been a turning point for both of them and while she missed her friend every day, their phone calls and video chats helped quell the sadness, and fill some of the time she used to spend with Sadie.

But enough with the sad thoughts. Time to get this show on the road or more aptly, her best friend down the aisle.

"It's time," Mel said, smiling at Sadie.

Laughing, Sadie answered, "About damn time!"

"Sadie," her mom scolded.

Giggling like a pair of teenagers, they led the way through the store.

Mel would precede Sadie and her mother down the aisle; Carly then her twin sister Laura would go before Mel. She liked Alex's cousins. She hadn't met their younger brothers yet but from what Carly and Laura said, she should count herself lucky.

Laura met them at the front door of the shop, where she waited with Bea Hargrove, the owner of Winter Lake Wears. Sucking in a breath she said, "Damn. I hope I don't have to arrest Alex on his wedding day."

Laughing, Sadie gave Laura a quick hug. "I'll make sure he behaves." Winking she added, "Or we'll find somewhere private."

"*Sadie*. You'll do no such thing," Sadie's mom chided.

Hoping to divert a lecture for her best friend, Mel asked, "Are we good to start?"

"Everyone and everything is in place," Laura said. "All we have to do is give the signal and Dad will start up the music."

"Then send the signal," Sadie answered, her mouth stretched in a brilliant smile.

Opening the door, Laura leaned out and did some complicated hand gesture which resulted in almost instantaneous music. With a grin, she turned back with a thumbs up. "Good to go."

Bea, decked out in a pink sequined tracksuit, took control of the door and held it wide. "Ladies," she said with a slight bow and an elaborate sweep of her arm.

One by one, Carly, Laura, and Mel exited the shop and walked the short distance across the street to the edge of the park where their corresponding groomsmen waited to escort them down the flower-petal sprinkled aisle.

With the way they'd set things up, Alex wouldn't be able to see Sadie until she arrived at the top of the aisle. He'd have an unobstructed view of his bride at that point because the bridal party would be in place at the bottom of the gazebo stairs before Sadie would leave the shop.

Mel tried to take everything in, tried to enjoy the moment, but by the time she reached Alex she realized it was fruitless. Already the previous minutes were a blur; she barely remembered John taking her hand when she'd reached the curb, never mind the walk down the aisle.

Smiling up at John, she let go of his arm and they each moved to their spots. As one the bridal party turned to look down the aisle to wait for the bride to arrive.

The music changed and Sadie appeared. Mel heard Alex suck in a sharp breath and quickly check whether the groom had fallen to his knees. He was still on his feet but his legs were definitely shaking.

Gasps, oos, ahs, and tears—the latter mainly from Alex—

followed Sadie down the aisle. When her best friend reached the gazebo stairs Alex took her hand and pulled it to his lips.

"That was close. I almost had to call for oxygen," he murmured, his eyes glued to Sadie's face.

Sadie laughed and Mel smiled. She was privy to the inside joke only because she'd begged Sadie for every detail of Alex's proposal.

"Are we ready? Or do you two need a moment?" Harry Windburn, Winter Lake's mayor, asked with a chuckle.

"We're ready," Sadie and Alex said together as they took the stairs up into the gazebo where Harry waited.

The rest of the wedding party followed, each taking a step to form a kind of honor guard during the ceremony.

Mel looked out at the gathered crowd. She knew some of the faces from her week in town, but most were strangers to her, but obviously not to Alex or Sadie.

It seemed as though the whole population of Winter Lake had shown up to watch their hometown boy marry.

Laura growled under her breath behind Mel. Turning slightly, she asked in a whisper, "What's wrong?"

"Our brother's friends are here."

"And? So's the rest of town and a good number of tourists by the looks of it," Mel pointed out.

"Yes, but the town and tourists aren't a bunch of meat-headed college football players only looking for a good time."

Mel glanced in the direction Laura scowled and took in the group of young men. They were around twenty years old if she were to guess, and she couldn't help admiring them.

Watching them reminded her of her college days and the football players who hung out in the green space between the dorms.

If they stuck around for the rest of the festivities maybe she could score a dance with one or two of the hotties. She'd steer clear of Laura and Carly's brother though. No point muddying that water. Especially if she got extra lucky and did a little more than dancing.

"Alex and Sadie." Harry's voice brought Mel back to the moment and her maid-of-honor duties. "As you take this new step in your journey through life, we thank you for allowing us to be part of this special day."

Mel smiled at the couple in front of her.

She wanted that. Wanted to give herself to a man who would give himself in return. And while there was a little envy that Sadie had found that with Alex, Mel didn't begrudge her friend happiness.

She might not have found the guy for her yet but she would.

One day.

CHAPTER 1

MIAMI - THREE YEARS LATER

Tipping back her head and opening her mouth, Melinda Shaw dropped the tablet to the back of her throat and swallowed.

Tick, tick, tick, tick.

"Stupid biological clock. Damn thing wasn't even working a day ago," Mel grumbled as she tossed her contraceptive packet in the drawer. It was the last one. She'd have to stop at the pharmacy and get a prescription filled.

"It's all Sadie's fault. If she wasn't glowing with marital bliss and sharing all the wonderful delights of being a domestic goddess, I wouldn't feel like I'm missing something. Like life is passing me by."

She headed for the front door.

"Thirty isn't old."

It wasn't. Except...

It *felt* old.

Sighing, Mel grabbed the handle of her rolling crate and opened the door. She pushed through the wall of heat that greeted her and cursed the need to go out on this scorching summer day. She'd been more than ready to tackle the day until her best friend had called.

"So what if Sadie has been married three years already. So what if she's now pregnant and moving into the next stage of her life. A stage we'd always planned to do together." Mel huffed out a breath. "It's not like I've got anyone to get pregnant with anyway. Or the time to raise a family."

Mel hit the button on her car key to pop the trunk. With a grunt, she lifted the crate inside and used the straps conveniently located on the right side of the storage space to secure the box that held everything she needed to make it through today's event.

"It's not a race. And really, I don't need a guy to have a baby."

She frowned.

"Okay, fine. *Technically* I need a guy, but it's not like I need him to stick around for diaper changes or midnight feedings."

She slammed the trunk closed.

"But I want him to," she whispered.

Staring blindly through the back window of her car, she swallowed over the lump in her throat and pressed a hand to the ache in her chest.

"I want both dammit. I want what Sadie has."

Mel rolled her eyes.

"Jesus. Listen to me."

Shaking her head, she moved around the car to the driver's door and pulled it open.

"Sadie gets pregnant and I turn into a whiny female. She's supposed to be the hormonal one, not me!"

Leaving the door open, Mel sank into the overheated interior and tried not to breathe in the stale, hot air. Shoving the key in the ignition, she cranked the engine and waited for the AC to kick in.

Already sweat coated her skin from the short walk to her car. Her work pants and shirt clung to the dampness and she had the whole day to get through yet.

When cold air finally blasted from the vents, she closed the door and put her seat belt on. No point bitching about the weather when she couldn't control it.

"What I *can* control is my life and how I look at it. I'm a professional success. It's taken a few years but I'm the owner of Miami's most sought-after event management firm. *And my house is almost paid off, only two more payments to go; that's a personal success right there.*"

She put the car in gear and reversed out of her driveway.

"It doesn't matter that Sadie has two things I want. Just because I don't have them now doesn't mean I won't in the future."

It didn't take long—or much concentration—to navigate the light traffic in her neighborhood.

"Still plenty of time to find Mr. Right."

In minutes, she was turning onto the main road that would take her to the venue for today's event.

Storm Arena.

Home of the Miami Storm football team.

Mel grinned.

"A day filled with enough eye candy to make a girl wetter than the heat wave currently gripping the city."

She thought about all the prime male specimens who filled the roster of the Storm football team—

The blare of her ringtone tore through the car and her yummy thoughts. A quick glance showed a name and number she really didn't want to think about today. Or any other day.

"You've got a nerve, asshole." She glared through the windshield at the car in front of her. "You seriously think I'm going to pick up after finding you balls deep in that twenty-something intern?"

Mel checked her mirrors and changed lanes, the ringtone continuing to blast through her speakers.

"You're a stupid bastard if you think I'll talk to you ever again."

She let the call go to voice mail but had no intention of listening later. She'd delete the message and block the contact while she was at it.

Rodney Michaels was the last man she wanted to think about. Especially when contemplating her lack of significant other and children. She couldn't believe she'd thought he was a good candidate as a partner and father.

"The world is full of toads. Well, Miami is at least. God knows I've kissed more than my share over the years. Especially recently."

Taking her exit, she merged with the cars heading in the direction of the arena.

Family Day for the players and staff of the Miami Storm wouldn't start for another few hours but already there would be numerous employees and—hopefully—her staff onsite.

Everything was in place; she'd made sure of that before leaving the venue at 1am this morning.

This event was slated to be their best this year. Barring any unforeseen issues...

"Nope. Not going there. Nothing will go wrong today."

Mel pulled up to the gate behind a minivan and a catering truck. Reaching for her bag, she searched for her ID.

When she stopped beside the guard, he took her license with a smile. He checked it against the clipboard in his hand before giving it back. "Have a good day, ma'am."

Her smile wobbled as she grabbed her license and

dropped it in her lap. *Ma'am? What happened to Miss?* When the boom gate lifted she drove through, a frown on her face.

"Do I look like a ma'am?" she muttered while searching for a spot close to the door she would use to enter the arena. "It's bad enough I suddenly feel old. Now apparently I look it."

Nosing her car into the space between a small yellow hatchback and a black monster SUV, Mel's frown deepened.

"Oh my God. I'm talking to myself. Having complete conversations. Nobody else needed."

Switching off the engine, she lowered her head to the wheel, banging it twice.

"No wonder I can't find a decent guy. I'm not just getting old; I'm going insane along with it."

A tap next to her made her jump; her head snapped up, a tiny squeak leaving her throat along with the contents of her lungs.

Slamming a hand over her pounding heart she turned to find her assistant, Carla, smiling at her through the window.

A smile that seemed a little strained around the edges, kind of manic really.

Instantly Mel knew it wasn't going to be a good a day and she wasn't sure she wanted to get out of the car.

With a bad feeling in her belly, she scooped up her bag and phone. Putting her ID away, she plastered on a smile and opened the door.

"And the day begins," she muttered and stepped out into the thick Miami heat.

CHAPTER 2

GRADY CAME out of the tunnel and smiled. Nothing beat the thrill of coming out of the dark into the light, and he breathed deep, surveying the scene in front of him.

Storm Family Day.

It was surreal to see the stadium set up this way. Normally nothing covered the grass except the painted white lines of the gridiron. Today that field was hidden beneath a carnival to rival any state fair he'd been to.

Rides, food stalls, sideshow games...hell, there was even a house of horrors and a miniature Ferris wheel.

It made him homesick for the Ice Breaker Festival his hometown put on every year.

When was the last time he'd been home for that? The last year of high school?

He was ashamed to admit he hadn't made the trek home nearly enough since he'd packed his bags and headed to Miami on a full-ride football scholarship.

Shaking off the guilt he stepped forward. The place was already packed. Noise that rivaled any home game he attended surrounded him and there were adults and kids everywhere.

A pre-teen barreled into his side. Laughing, the kid shot him an apologetic wave then took off into the crowd, with two other boys around the same age close on his heels. The last one wore a Storm jersey with the number ten on the back.

Grady grinned. Nothing better than seeing a fan wearing not only your team colors, but your number too. With a smile on his face, he moved deeper into the crowd.

He waved at players and Storm staff he knew well, nodded at those he didn't know so well but smiled his way, and in spite of the homesickness this event inspired, was grateful to be here.

It was his second year with the Storm and while he was no longer a rookie, he still wasn't quite *one of them* yet. But he would be. He'd make sure of it.

He felt good and he'd be getting more game time this year. He'd passed the test so to speak in his first few starts last season but this year would see him cement his position—his place—with the team.

See him prove he was worth that big-money contract.

He'd performed well during training camp. And with Foley's injury, Grady was guaranteed a start in the first games of the season. He just needed to make sure he played outstandingly so the coaches would think twice about pulling him from the starting lineup when Foley's ankle was no longer a concern.

"Hey, Grade A!"

Grady smiled at the nickname his teammates had given him when he first signed on, and turned to see Garrett Sandler heading his way. "Hey."

They shook hands. Did a half-hug, shoulder-slap, back pound thing. "Ready?"

"For?" Grady asked.

The running back nodded in the direction of a...shit, was that a pie-eating contest?

He shook his head. "Ah...no. I'll pass." He was a fan of pie—hell, his big sister Carly made the best pumpkin pie on the planet—but he preferred to savor his dessert. One yummy bite at a time not one whole pie at a time.

Garrett laughed. "C'mon, man, I've seen you eat."

He chuckled, tipping his chin at the lineup of contestants. "I think I'll leave it to the kids."

"Yeah, well, you know we've got a couple of big kids on the team."

They watched as three of the Storm's tackles moved behind the table lined with what looked like cream pies. The teenagers already there razzed them and he watched as some good natured trash talk went down for a few minutes before a guy with a staff vest on brought them all back to the task at hand and they all took a seat.

"Jesus." Grady asked. "They're serious?"

"Yep." Garrett made the p pop. "They do it every year."

Grady shook his head as the whistle sounded and eight heads bent, mouths open, and began to devour filling and pastry in anything but a polite manner. He couldn't help laughing as faces were quickly covered with cream from chin to forehead and ear to ear.

Garrett nudged him with his shoulder. "I'm going to head over to the food area, you coming?"

"Sure. Although I think I just lost my appetite."

"Wait 'til you see what they've got set up over here. You'll change your mind in a heartbeat. I swear, it's exactly like the county fair back home in Ohio. My grandparents used to take us every year," Garrett said as they weaved their way through the crowd.

"It *is* pretty bizarre considering what's normally here when we come out of the tunnel."

Grady bumped into a woman about a foot shorter than him. Hands snapping out, he wrapped them around her upper arms to steady her and was hit with a vision of dark hair, smooth skin, and crystal-clear blue eyes.

"Sorry," he murmured, his gaze riveted to that sweep of dark hair partially obscuring her face.

She smiled at him absently, shook her arms to get him to let go, then disappeared around a group of teens lining up to try their luck at shooting ducks before he could get another word out or a better look at her.

But there was no denying the punch of lust that had slammed into his gut when his fingers had touched her silky-smooth skin.

Being six-four in normal circumstances would mean he'd be head and shoulders above everyone else and could easily follow someone through a crowd, but not here.

Here, he was but one of many giants, and even standing on his toes, craning his neck, he quickly lost sight of the mystery woman.

"Hey, you coming or not?" Garrett called out.

"Sure." Dropping down on his heels, Grady shook his head and followed his teammate.

They reached the first food stall in a long row of them and Grady's senses were assaulted with the sights and smells of his youth.

Corn dogs, cotton candy, funnel cakes, popcorn, and the unmistakable scent of all things fried. He took a deep breath.

God, he'd missed this. He really needed to see about going home next year for the Ice Breaker Festival.

Mouth watering, he rubbed his hands together and said, "All right. Let's get started."

"Sweet or savory?" Garrett asked.

Grady arched one eyebrow at him.

"Right, right. Stupid question. Both it is."

Laughing, they joined the line for corn dogs.

Grady reached into his pocket for the wad of cash he'd been hoarding in preparation for today.

Storm management were footing the bill for the whole event but they'd suggested a donation for anything you did or consumed, which would go into the fund the team used to sponsor various charities throughout the district.

Grady thought it was a brilliant idea and had been putting money away since the coach had mentioned this year's theme at the start of training camp. He had over a grand in dollar bills to spend.

He figured it would take him at least two hundred to get through the food stalls. Once his stomach was full, he'd head for the rides, or possibly the sideshows.

Not that it mattered. He had all day to wander around and spend his cash.

CHAPTER 3

"Fuck." Mel kept the curse under her breath due to the numerous children running around when what she really wanted to do was scream it at the top of her lungs and throw things.

Lots and lots of things.

"I'm sure we could—"

"Do you have any mechanical knowledge, Carla?" Mel glared at her assistant.

"Um, well, no, but—"

Mel held up her hand to stop anything else coming out of Carla's mouth. She didn't mean to be rude or disrespectful but she needed to think and at this point neither of them were voicing any sane answers to their problem.

Taking a deep breath, she scanned the area. Who the hell could help her get this thing fixed? She'd already called the guy who owned and operated the rides she'd hired for the day but the call had gone straight to voice mail.

Not only was *he* unavailable, the man he'd left in charge to keep an eye on everything had disappeared and the attendant was just some college student who didn't know the inner workings of the Ferris wheel, only which button to push to start and which to push to stop.

She was pissed off on so many levels. And her anger shouldn't be aimed at her right-hand man—or woman in this case. "Sorry, Carla, I just need a minute."

Carla smiled. "Nothing to apologize for. I've got nothing of value to add on this dilemma but I'm trying to come up with something anyway."

Mel returned her smile. Neither of them were used to having a problem they couldn't deal with and this wasn't the first disaster to strike today. Luckily the others had been within their skillset and easily fixed. This one not so much. Or not at all.

She blew out a breath.

Mark Mitchum was going to have a fit over this debacle, and while she wasn't scared of the man, she was definitely worried what this would do to her rep and future work.

Melinda Shaw had a reputation for pulling off the impossible—and she'd promised the Storm president a Ferris wheel.

A disaster like this could see Shaw Events tumble from the top spot in event management.

There was no point worrying about it now.

Damage control.

She had to shut down the Ferris wheel indefinitely and pray Mr. Derwood returned her call soon. Or his supervising employee turned up.

Oh. And get on her knees and thank God no one was stuck on the damn thing.

"What should we do?" Carla asked.

"Not much we can do, unfortunately." Turning to the attendant, Mel said, "I'll need you to stay here until the day is over even though you won't actually be doing anything. Tell

Carla what you want food and drink wise and she'll get it for you, and she'll check back from time to time to make sure you're okay. Oh, and call Carla the second your boss shows up. Carla, give him your number."

"Sure. No worries." The boy—Mel didn't even know his name—pulled his phone from his pocket and punched in Carla's number then he parked his butt on the grass in front of the now useless control panel, his gaze glued to his phone.

Dammit. The biggest draw of the carnival was out of commission. She needed something else exciting to replace it.

"Hey, something wrong?"

Mel turned and looked up, up—waaay up—into eyes so gold they rivaled the sun. She'd never seen eyes that color before. And like the sun, they momentarily blinded her to everything else.

"Hello?" He waved a hand in front of her face. "You okay?"

She blinked. "I, um..." She'd been out in the heat too long. What else could explain the sudden flash-fire under her skin, the lack of air in her lungs?

"Can I help?" He nodded at the ride behind her. "I've got a knack for all things mechanical."

"Oh. Thanks, but I don't think I can let anyone touch it." She shrugged. "Insurance and liability and all that. Plus the owner would probably have an issue with someone messing with it."

"Need help with anything else?"

Who was this guy? "I don't think so. But thank you for the offer."

"Want some water?" He held up a bottle.

Mel stared at him while her brain tried to process his question.

"You're looking a little flushed. It's really hot out here. Thought you could use some cooling off." He grinned.

My God, that smile. More heat licked through her, and her lower belly pulsed, tightened. She was the first to admit she'd been around the block a time or two, so she knew when a guy was interested. And this guy was. If the look in his eyes was any indication, he was more than interested.

He cracked the lid on the bottle then held it out. "Here."

Reflexes had her taking the water and bringing it to her mouth. She watched him watch her. Those gold eyes flared as she pursed her lips around the bottle and tipped it up. She swallowed a mouthful and his Adam's apple bobbed, his tongue slipping out and taking a slow sensuous trip across his full bottom lip.

She took several soothing gulps—because suddenly her mouth and throat were bone dry and her body felt like it was on fire—before handing the water back. "Thanks," she croaked.

He grinned. "You're welcome."

"I..." All thought left her head when the hunk of masculine perfection in front of her brought the bottle to his mouth and drank.

God, the man had a gorgeous mouth. Lips thick enough to get your attention and hold it. The idea of those lips pressed to hers—cruising over her body—had her heart rate accelerating and her breath stuttering.

He grinned wide again and held out his hand. "I'm Grady."

Mel put her hand in his, hers immediately swallowed up as he curled his fingers around it, and shook. "Mel."

"*Mel.*" He seemed to test the weight, the taste of her name on his tongue. "Well, Mel, you're probably going to need something to distract everyone from the non-functioning Ferris wheel. Why don't I round up a few of the guys and a ball and start a game to occupy anyone who's thinking about riding this thing?"

"Are you for real?" She'd been lamenting Miami's lack of princes only a few hours ago and now she was faced with a guy willing to go out of his way to help her.

A real-life Prince Charming? He couldn't be real.

Maybe she *had* been out in the heat too long. Perhaps she'd passed out from heat stroke and was hallucinating.

She was contemplating poking him in the stomach when he did something that proved just how real he was.

He leaned toward her, dipped his head until his mouth was near her ear, his warm breath fanning over her neck, and murmured, "I'm as real as it gets—and you'll know that to your very bones before I'm done."

Struck dumb, Mel gaped as he turned and walked away.

CHAPTER 4

KNOWING Mel watched him walk away put a grin on his face.

He hadn't realized he'd been keeping an eye out for his mystery woman until he'd spotted her by the Ferris wheel. And when he did, it was the same as before.

A kick to the gut—the tightening of muscles, the hardening of places that really shouldn't be hardening here.

He needed to get her somewhere private so he could put his hands on her. His lips. Press his body against hers.

He needed...

He needed to give himself a slap.

What he needed was to rein in those urges until they weren't surrounded by his team mates and their kids, his coaches.

The president of the fucking club!

When he put his hands on her again it wouldn't be where anyone could see them. They'd be alone with no risk of interruption. And he had every intention of making that happen before the end of the day.

For now he needed a distraction from his lusty thoughts,

and getting a few of his teammates to help him put together a game would be just the thing.

He spotted Garrett and waved. Jogging over, Grady nodded at the other players standing with the running back. "Hey, wanna start up a game?"

"Sure," Garrett answered. "You know if we just throw a ball around, they'll come."

Grady grinned. "Anyone got a ball?"

"I've got one," a gangly teen spoke up beside him, a well-used football in his hands. "My dad gave it to me."

The kid looked vaguely familiar. "Great," Grady said.

"Game on." Sawyer, one of Storm's cornerbacks, pumped a fist in the air.

Smiling, Grady nodded at the kid. "Got any friends who might want to throw the ball around with us?"

"For sure."

"Round them up and meet us behind the Ferris wheel." Grady pointed to the large grass area behind the broken ride.

"I'll get my dad too," the kid said.

Grady arched an eyebrow at Garrett as the kid took off. "The Wall's kid."

Defense. Grady rubbed his hands together. Looked like they had a ball game. "Okay. Let's do this."

Grady was amazed at how quickly a little game turned into a big one. Within ten minutes of the first pass, there were more than the regulation eleven players on each team and spectators three and four deep on the sideline, cheering everyone on.

Most of the Storm players were actually coaching the kids on the field. The rules were incidental to the teaching of skills. By the time Coach Bane wandered into the middle of the game with whistle to mouth, Grady had worked up a sweat.

Coach got them into a vague semblance of order and play resumed, until Jax Elliot picked up a little girl, her tiny arms wrapped around the ball in a death grip. With the girl snugged under his arm as though she were the football, Jax ran to the goal line for a touchdown. The game was forgotten as everyone cheered and laughed at the running back's antics and the little girl's squeals of joy.

When Lexi Mitchum walked out to retrieve the girl, Grady couldn't help but smile. And if there was a twinge of envy when Mark Mitchum reached the two females and wrapped his arms around them both, then Grady would just have to work harder on getting everything he wanted.

He'd reached several life goals so far. And now that his football career was on solid ground, he could put a little more effort into his personal life.

His smile widened when he spotted a certain dark-haired beauty watching from the sideline. Things were already looking up in that area.

"Hey." Garrett shoulder-bumped him. "Who you checking out?"

"Huh?" Grady turned to see his teammate scanning the spectators. "No one in particular."

"Good thing. You shouldn't fish where you work, man. Too complicated when you toss them back." Garrett's words rang with experience.

Grady shrugged. "Not looking to fish at all."

It was a lie, but one his friend would accept without question because Grady wasn't like most of the other single players in the league. He wasn't a player off the field. Never had been. And being a well-paid football star, with women readily available and willing to be his, hadn't changed his dating code.

He'd never had a one-night stand.

His gaze tracked back to Mel.

He might have to rethink his view on meaningless flings though, if it meant getting her between his sheets.

Except if the punch of lust he felt whenever he thought of her was anything to go by, meaningless was the last thing they'd be.

He'd cross that bridge when he came to it. First things first. He had to come up with a way to spend time with her. Away from prying eyes.

"C'mon." He clapped Garrett on the back. "Let's play."

He played hard but was mindful of doing anything stupid. No point risking injury in a friendly game. Sweat still dripped off him when Coach Bane finally called it quits. The sun was setting and a few of the younger kids were asleep on blankets or a parent's lap.

Grady glanced around and felt the warmth of satisfaction seep through him. He'd not just found a team to play for when the Storm drafted him. He'd found a family he wanted to be part of—*was* part of.

"Grady?"

He turned to find Mel staring up at him. Grady smiled. "Hey."

"I want to say thank you." She held out an open bottle of water.

"For?" Grabbing the bottle, he gulped down half of it without taking a breath.

"Stopping today from turning into a complete disaster."

Grady's smile widened. "There was no chance of that."

"Oh no, if you hadn't come up with the football game idea, we would have had a big hole with the Ferris wheel out of commission. I owe you."

He stepped closer. Towered over her. "You owe me?"

"I, ah—"

"Have dinner with me."

"What?"

"Dinner."

"Dinner?"

"Yes. You. Me. Table. Food." He grinned. Flustering her was kind of fun. She didn't strike him as the type to fluster easily. Good to know he could manage it. "Tonight."

"Oh. Well." She glanced at the iPad in her hand. "I probably won't be finished here before ten."

It wasn't a refusal. "Works for me. I need to shower first anyway. Wash all this sweat off my body."

He loved the way a flush crept up her neck and into her cheeks when he talked about showering. His fingers seemed to have a mind of their own because he was brushing the tips across that color without thought.

"Why don't I cook for you?" he asked. The idea of her in his house—at his table—filling him with pleasure.

"You can cook?"

He chuckled at her obvious disbelief. "Yeah, catching the ball isn't my only skill." Grady winked and put enough inflection in his voice to let her know he had many skills he wanted to share with her.

Her blush deepened and before she could reject his invitation, he handed her the water and grabbed her iPad. He quickly added his address and phone number to her contacts.

Handing the device back, he said, "See you after you're done here."

He walked away without looking back. She might not have said yes, but she hadn't said no either. Her silence implied acceptance. He banked on her being too polite to not show up so if she wanted to cancel, she'd have to call him.

At which point he'd have her number and a way to stay in touch.

CHAPTER 5

Mel took the turn onto Grady's street and muttered, "What the hell am I doing?"

She should have said no back at Storm Arena when he'd asked her to dinner. Should have called and said no at some point in the last few hours. Or at least sent a text saying she couldn't make it.

Except every time she picked up her phone to call or text, her fingers wouldn't work.

Since she'd met Grady, her brain hadn't worked all that well either. All she could think about was getting him naked.

The man had her hot and bothered without even touching her, and it was more stimulation than she'd had lately. Her most recent sex had been with a guy who'd shown more enthusiasm for sticking his dick in a young intern's ass.

Of course, the fact the intern was a guy might have had something to do with Rod's level of exuberance, his...

"Shit. Not going there," she growled. Putting a brake on her thoughts as she put her foot on the brake of her car, she glanced through the side window and slammed her foot to the floor. "Holy fuck!"

The house she'd stopped in front of could only be described as a mansion. Compared to her place, anyway. It probably wasn't quite billionaires' row, but *damn* it was close. Very, very close.

Just who the hell was Grady?

He might do it for her—in a big way—but she wasn't about to knock on his front door without knowing a little bit more about the man. Grabbing her iPad, she pulled up his contact details and read his last name.

Murdock.

Grady Murdock...

"Why does that name ring a bell?"

Opening a browser, Mel typed in "Grady Murdock" and watched as link after link popped up.

"Wow."

Tapping on the first one, she quickly scanned the article. Okay, the guy—shit, he was only twenty-four—was some kind of superstar football player.

"Crap."

Two years ago he was a top draft pick.

That must be why his name rang a bell.

Twenty-four.

"Double crap."

Six years younger than her.

Why did that make her feel like a dirty old woman?

She wasn't old. Not even middle-aged. But Grady was barely out of college. Still, it wasn't like he was underage or anything as bad as that...

"And he looks older than twenty-four," she mused while eyeing the photos accompanying the article.

Damn, he looked amazing in his uniform. The pants

hugged his thighs and ass like a second skin.

"He's an adult. Has a five-year contract with the Miami Storm reported to be worth over twenty million."

She double-clicked to enlarge one of the photos of Grady on the field. *Damn, that ass.*

"He could have dinner with any woman he wanted. Just because I'm older than he is doesn't mean jack. Besides, it's not like I'm planning to marry the guy."

Leaning in, Mel tried to determine if that was padding or...

"What the fuck am I doing? Why am I rationalizing this? We're both single, consenting adults. So what if he's in his twenties and I'm in my thirties... Jesus. I'm a cougar in the making."

Turning the iPad off, she shoved it in her bag and debated taking her foot off the brake and driving away.

She didn't get the chance.

One of the triple-garage doors lifted and, ducking underneath, Grady came out with a wide grin and a wave. He jogged down the driveway, those sculptured thighs flexing.

"Can't leave now," she muttered as she hit the button to lower the passenger window.

Crouching beside her car, he leaned in the window, the smile on his face infectious. "Park in the garage. There have been a few cars vandalized in recent weeks."

Her smile dimmed. "Vandalized?" Mel glanced around the affluent suburb where not a blade of grass appeared out of place, never mind a slash of graffiti marring the pristine residences.

He smiled that knee-melting smile that kicked up her pulse and wet her in places that made her squirm. "Egged. Kids probably, and harmless really, but I'd prefer not to have to wash your car," he explained.

"I won't be here that long..."

He was shaking his head and saying, "No point risking it."

She could understand the logic. She could. What she couldn't understand was her reluctance to do it. Parking out of harm's way made perfect sense. The last thing she wanted to be doing was scraping dried egg off her paintwork and windows.

And if it were anyone else—other than an axe murderer—making the suggestion, she'd readily agree.

Except Grady Murdock had her senses reeling and her wits scattering.

Just the sight of him in his running shorts and fitted t-shirt had her whole body on alert.

The shorts revealed long legs thick with muscles that, according to the article she'd just read, made him one of the fastest men in the league. And the way his shirt molded to his pecs, his six-pack abs, told her he didn't neglect other parts of his body in favor of those powerful thighs.

She couldn't see it now but she couldn't forget about his ass either—god, he had the tightest ass.

Mel swallowed. Her throat dry and tight with arousal, she had to clear it to speak. "O-okay."

He grinned at her, patted the window frame, and said, "See you inside."

It took her a moment to remove her foot from the brake and turn into his driveway.

Hard to concentrate on anything other than the oh-so-fine ass that had her tongue hanging out as he walked toward the garage. His shorts fit just as snugly as his shirt and she'd be damned if she could pull her gaze away from those tight buns as they headed away from her.

Would Grady let her nibble on that ass? Would he object to a lick or two?

"Shit, Melinda, snap out of it. You're here for dinner. That's it." She watched him disappear into the garage and drew in a big breath. "Maybe."

Easing her foot off the brake, she got moving. As she pulled into Grady's garage, she had to be honest. Being here had nothing to do with the fact she hadn't eaten since lunch and needed a meal.

She was here because she couldn't stay away.

If nothing else, she had to admit that Grady Murdock drew her in a way she hadn't felt in…years, if ever. His age—her age—didn't matter. This was about sexual attraction—chemistry, biology, pheromones. Pure and simple. Mel wanted to fuck Grady.

Hard and all night.

One look at him waiting for her had her insides quivering. When was the last time a guy had her revved so high? She wasn't stupid, didn't indulge in one-night stands—not anymore.

Except Grady made her want to go back to those wild days of college where she'd screw anything that caught her fancy.

She'd always taken control of her sexuality and wasn't ashamed of it. She'd never been reckless or stupid or indiscriminate, but if she liked a guy enough to go after him, she did.

Of course, no one these days ever really got her attention.

No one apparently except a twenty-four-year-old, football-playing superstar.

She'd give herself one night—if that's where he wanted to take them—to indulge in every sexual pleasure Grady and his mouthwatering body offered.

One night.

Then she'd walk away.

CHAPTER 6

GRADY WASN'T sure what had happened between the street and the garage, except Mel seemed more...open? Yeah, that was it. She was more open, less guarded.

And definitely happy to be here.

"I hope you're not a vegetarian," he said as he led her into his house. He hadn't had time to ask earlier.

"No way in hell." She grinned at him. "I'm far too fond of meat for that."

He ignored the innuendo in her words, the spark of it in her eyes as she swept them down his body, and asked, "How do you like your steak?"

"Medium." She placed her bag on the counter separating his kitchen and living area. Pulling out a stool, she perched on the edge. "What can I do to help?"

"Nothing. Potatoes are done. Same with the salad." He pulled the tray of meat from the oven. "Do you want a drink?"

"Don't suppose you have any wine?"

He smiled. "I do. I keep it for when my mom or sisters visit. Anything in particular you prefer?"

"I'm easy as long as it's white and cold." Mel hopped off the stool and came around into the kitchen. "Let me get it. I feel funny sitting there letting you wait on me."

Grady handed her the bottle he'd selected from the fridge. "Corkscrew is in the second drawer over there and glasses are in the cupboard there."

"Are you having some?"

"Nah." He tipped his head, indicting the bottle on the counter. "I've got a beer."

"Oh." She frowned. "Maybe I'll have one of those instead."

"Sure. Help yourself to whatever you want. I'm going to put these steaks on the grill. Join me out on the patio when you've got your drink." Grady grabbed his beer and left the house through the open bi-fold doors that ran the length of his living room.

He liked seeing Mel in his kitchen. Really liked watching her park her car beside his SUV in the garage. Now if he could just see her in his bed...

One step at a time. She'd accepted his invitation to dinner and he had to woo her with his cooking skills and sparkling personality before he thought about getting naked.

Smiling, he forked the meat onto the grill. He'd fired it up earlier so it was at the perfect temp for searing the steaks. They'd only take a minute each side. In no time, he'd be enjoying a nice meal with an attractive woman.

Something he hadn't done in what felt like forever.

If he was honest, he hadn't wanted to. He wasn't a fan of the football groupies and he'd been concentrating on his career so much that he hadn't done anything, gone anywhere, to meet any new women.

He wanted one who wouldn't see him as just Grade A of the Miami Storm, but as Grady Murdock, a guy who wanted what his parents had. A partnership that spanned a lifetime, that formed the foundation a loving family could grow from.

He hadn't met anyone who he could see himself doing that with.

Mel walked out onto the patio with beer bottle in hand.

Until now.

This one he wanted to know. In every way. Wanted to see if what he felt was the beginning of such a connection.

"Tell me about event coordinating," he said as Mel took a seat at the table beside the grill.

She lifted one shoulder. "Not much to tell. Clients tell me what they want and I make it happen."

He chuckled. "I think it's a little more complex than that."

"Probably." She put her bottle on the table. "But can I be honest?"

"Sure."

"After the day I've had, I'd rather not talk about my work."

"Okay." He flipped the steaks. "What's your favorite movie?"

"What?" Her beer was back in her hand but she held it in midair as she eyed him. "Favorite movie? Why?"

"I'm asking."

"Ah, okay." She nodded. "Movie: Anything with a good story, a happy ending, and no, I don't mean *that* kind of happy ending." She laughed before continuing. "Book: Don't get time to read but when I do, I'm partial to romance, the hotter the better and definitely with *that* kind of happy ending. Food: Hot, buttered popcorn. Totally my weakness. Weather: Again, hot but not as hot as it's been in recent days. Color: Used to be blue but I've suddenly got a thing for gold."

Grady smirked. "Are you rushing things?"

"Grady, we met a few hours ago and I'm already at your

house. I think we passed rushing a while back." She took a sip of beer. "We could move to warp speed."

"Oh?"

Mel leaned back in her chair, the beer bottle dangling from one hand. "More honesty. I think we're both on the same page, so it's safe to say this dinner and conversation are moving toward the bedroom and sex."

His hand jerked, the steak he'd picked up to put on the plate almost getting tossed in the air. "Honesty," he mumbled.

"You don't need to wine and dine me to get me into bed, Grady."

He stared at her. "Fuck and be done?"

"If that's what you want."

Grady had no intention of accepting so little of her. "And if I want more?"

"Like what?" She tilted her head to the side, seeming genuinely perplexed by the thought.

"A nice evening spending time with a more-than-nice woman who I happen to want to get out of her pants."

"No dinner, no sex?" she asked, a frown marring her pretty face.

Grady thought about it. Neither was dependent on the other. He wanted both. With her. "Didn't say that. But the steaks are ready and it seems a shame to waste this prime cut of beef, and after the day you've had, I'm sure you're hungry."

She smiled. "You've got me there. I'm definitely hungry and those steaks do smell good."

"Wait 'til you taste them."

"As long as steak isn't the only thing I'll be tasting before the night's over."

He watched as she brought her beer to her lips and wrapped them around the top. His groin throbbed, his cock hardening to almost full length.

He'd sported a semi for hours—since he'd bumped into her—and now that they were talking about sex, he was in danger of starving his brain of oxygen because all his blood was pooling between his legs.

Grady was ready to admit this woman could probably teach him a thing or two in the bedroom. She gave off a sexual hum that said she knew what the hell she was doing, what she wanted, and wasn't afraid to go after it.

And it seemed what she wanted was him.

CHAPTER 7

"SHE DID NOT," Mel exclaimed, the bottle in her hand forgotten.

"She totally did." Grady grinned.

"Your mom really did that?" she asked through her laughter. She put the beer back on the table so she didn't spill it.

"I couldn't make this stuff up." Obviously remembering, he shook his head with a rueful smile. "My brother and I never put itching powder in our sisters' beds again. Or anywhere else."

Her cheeks hurt. Her stomach ached.

Mel couldn't remember the last time she'd smiled so much. Laughed so much.

Grady Murdock was proving to be more interesting and entertaining, more attractive, with every second they spent together.

Getting her mirth under control enough to speak, she said, "Your mother is an extremely smart woman."

"Yes. She is."

"Either that, or evil. Very, very evil," Mel added with a smirk.

Chuckling, he said, "I think when you're trying to herd two preteen boys and a pair of hormonal teenage princesses, you'd have to be a little of both."

"Guess so, but still..." The thought of twelve-year-old Grady and his younger brother having to walk around in underwear covered in itching powder for a whole day made her giggle again. "She's a genius."

"I'm going to let you get away with that laugh because when I look back, it *is* kind of funny. Although at the time..." He shuddered, his sexy ass twisting a little in his seat.

Mel pulled her lips between her teeth and swallowed more laughter.

Grady eyed her. Leaning forward, he rested his arms on the table in front of him, and said, "All right, your turn."

"My turn?"

"Yeah, tell me something funny you did when you were a kid."

She turned over her memories and frowned. "I don't have any funny stories."

Raised by strict grandparents after her mother died, Mel remembered a very serious household where God and her grandfather ruled.

There were no games, no afternoons at the park, or anything that wasn't church or school related. She'd been five when her mom was killed in an accident; she barely remembered the woman.

And her father hadn't been in the picture before her mom had died, never mind after.

Shrugging, she said, "I don't recall there being all that much fun when I was growing up. Being an only child raised by grandparents has its drawbacks." She didn't want to say any more than that. She'd moved on from that lonely life, from that lonely little girl.

Grady brushed his fingertips over the back of her hand. "That's sad."

She'd never been emotionally or physically abused but her childhood hadn't been exactly happy. She shoved back the less-than-pleasant memories and forced a smile. She didn't need his sympathy. She'd made her own happy memories. "Don't worry. I made up for it in college."

More than if she were honest. Once she'd been out from under her grandfather's roof—his control—she'd been able to discover her true nature. And she might have taken her exploration a step too far on more than one occasion but she'd never been completely reckless.

She smiled thinking about some of the things she'd gotten up to back in school.

His mouth kicked up on one end. "I bet you did. Tell me some of those stories."

"Why?" She didn't want to talk about college. It would just remind her of the fact that when she was starting college Grady wasn't even in high school.

"It's your turn," he prodded.

"Did we put the evening in reverse?" she asked.

He smiled. "No. But I'm still enjoying a lovely meal with a lovely woman."

Mel glanced at their plates. "The meal is finished."

Grady looked down. "So it is."

"So..." She couldn't explain her need to rush. It wasn't as though she wasn't enjoying his company. She was. Maybe too much. Which was probably why she was attempting to move them to the obvious next step.

"You're ready for dessert?" Grady asked.

"If dessert is you. Yes." She nodded. "Definitely."

He leaned back in his chair, steepling his fingers beneath his chin. "I'm not going anywhere. But I get the feeling you are."

"No. Not yet, anyway." She wasn't leaving until she'd gotten a taste of him.

"Not a fan of anticipation? A slow build?"

"Is that what this is? Foreplay?"

One of those wide shoulders rose, dropped. "I think every look, every word, every second we've had together has been foreplay."

"And we're hanging back because…?"

"I'm savoring every moment."

She pushed her chair back and stood. "Then let's make those moments more memorable."

Walking around the table, she put an extra swing in her step, rocked her hips, and pulled her shoulders back to thrust her breasts forward. Her nipples were hard knots pressing against her blouse. He couldn't miss them.

Their time together had kept her arousal on a low hum but the talk of foreplay had amped it up another gear, leaving her with no doubt as to where she wanted the night to go.

Bed. Grady's bed.

Pushing his chair back, he held out a hand and patted his knee with the other. Slipping her fingers through his, she straddled his lap and nestled her knees beside his hips, slowly lowering her ass to his thighs. "You're so hard," she whispered.

He chuckled. "Yeah. Harder in some places."

They both looked down.

Mel wasn't sure if the shudder that went through her at the sight of the large erection tenting his shorts was from anticipation or anxiety.

The man was big. And in proportion. And big. Everywhere.

Bringing her gaze back to his face, she met his molten-gold eyes. "I'll be honest, Grady. I want to fuck you. I want to lick and suck and devour every inch of you."

His throat worked as he swallowed, his nostrils flaring as he drew in a long breath that lifted his wide chest and tempted her hands to touch.

A temptation she couldn't resist.

She laid her hands—fingers splayed—on that broad expanse of hot muscle, the material of his shirt doing nothing to corral his heat.

"I haven't wanted anyone this much in a very long time and I'm a little afraid I'm not going to be at all civilized about it." She leaned forward, pressed her mouth to his. "Tell me you're good with that."

He tangled the fingers of one hand in her hair; the other hand gripped her hip, held her still. "Mel." He breathed her name into her mouth. "I'm good with anything you want."

Eyes on his, she demanded, "Then kiss me like you mean it."

CHAPTER 8

HE WANTED to take his time. Wanted to carve every nanosecond of their first kiss on his memory. Except one taste of Mel's mouth had Grady's heart slamming against his ribs, his cock throbbing in his shorts.

He wanted her now.

Rising to his feet, he gripped her ass in both hands and walked into the house. His mouth stayed fused to hers. He was pretty sure the heat they generated had melded their lips together, never to be separated.

She was soft in his arms, her body fluid against his. Her hard nipples pressed into his chest and her pussy rubbed against his abs as she rocked with every step he took.

They wouldn't make it to his bedroom.

Turning left, Grady placed her ass on the kitchen counter. "Gotta have you now," he growled as he tore his mouth from hers.

"Yes." Her nails scored his back through his t-shirt, hard enough he'd have marks. "Here."

"This is going to be over too quickly." He fumbled with

the button and zipper on her pants. "Shit. Not quick enough."

He moved back a fraction and Mel knocked his hands away and took over. While she wiggled out of her pants, Grady shoved his shorts down and freed his cock.

"Fuck." He fisted his hands, clenched his jaw. "Condom."

"Right here." She leaned to the side and grabbed her purse. "I've got one."

When she dumped the contents of her bag on the counter beside them and a row of foil packets fell out, he mumbled, "Or more."

Mel grinned at him. "Girl Scout motto. Always be prepared."

One side of his mouth kicked up. "I've a new fondness for Girl Scout types."

"Well, I've got a fondness for this." She wrapped her hand around his cock and squeezed, stroked. "But it's a little under-dressed for what I have in mind."

With a practiced skill that crossed his eyes, Mel sheathed his length. Every muscle from head to toe drew tight, the air seizing in his lungs. "*Fuck.*"

She laughed. "Yeah. That's the plan."

Grady had never been with a sexually aggressive woman but Mel's demands, her confidence and willingness to go after what she wanted, had him so turned-on he was afraid he'd come the second he sank inside her.

They needed to slow down. *He* needed to slow down. Take a minute to get her to the same level of desperation as him. Dropping to his knees, he pushed her thighs apart and buried his face in her pussy.

She was hot and sweet and tart and he'd be damned if he didn't want to keep his mouth on her for hours.

Next time.

He used his thumbs to peel her open so he could get at

the heart of her. Slick with arousal, her flesh slid against his tongue like the richest cream. And the hard knot of her clit pulsed between his lips, against his tongue, when he sucked it.

Mel's sexy whimpers and moans filled the room. Her hips rocked, driving her sweet pussy into his mouth as she sought her pleasure. The press of her fingers to his head shoved him deeper and he slipped a thumb inside her hot hole and increased the suction on her clit.

She gasped and moaned. Undulated her hips, rocking her pussy against him.

Grady loved the way Mel didn't hold back. She rode his face as though getting her off was the only reason he had a mouth. He could feel her body coil—tighten—and knew she was close to going over the edge.

He wanted his cock inside her when she did.

Moving his thumb to her clit, he got to his feet and lined himself up. He had to bend his knees to get the right position but once he did, he wasted no time taking her.

With one savage plunge, Grady sank to the root. His balls tucked up close to his groin in response and he knew this would be over in a flash.

There was no controlling the pounding rhythm his body demanded. He yanked himself out, slammed back in. Over and over. Thrusting in and out. Hard and fast. Plunging deep, deeper.

Determined to get them both there, he kept his thumb on her clit. Stroked and pressed and circled.

She went wild. Gasping for breath and clawing at his shoulders, she bucked against him, her hips meeting each piercing stroke of his cock, her inner walls squeezing him.

A cry tore from her throat. The sound raw and edged with triumph as her body exploded around him.

Grady had no hope of holding out against his own release.

It detonated low and deep with muscle-clenching spasms. His legs shook, his chest heaved. He closed his eyes tight against the flash of lights going off in his vision. A split second of sanity had him bracing his hands on the counter, locking his knees.

If it wasn't for that, he'd have sunk to the floor in a bone-less heap, and taken a limp Mel with him.

Her face was buried in the curve of his neck, her breath hot against his sweat-slicked skin.

The tight heat of her pussy continued to clamp and release his cock in spite of the fact they'd both just come hard enough to blow the roof off his house.

"Holy fucking shit."

Grady chuckled.

"No. Seriously." She panted against his throat. "Holy. Fucking. Shit."

"Yeah. Those words work."

"We are *so* doing that again."

He smiled into her hair. "No argument."

"Now." She flexed her hips.

"I'll need..." Actually, he was still hard. And throbbing. Jesus. He'd never been this turned-on.

"A bed. We'll need a bed for the next round."

Grady lifted her against his chest and turned toward his bedroom. But one step stopped him. His pants were wrapped around his ankles.

Getting a tighter grip on Mel, he kicked out of his shorts and flicked them away.

"I hope you're not planning on leaving any time soon," he said as he made his way through the house.

"Nope."

"Good. Because once I get you in my bed, I'm not letting you out."

CHAPTER 9

GRADY'S BEDROOM wasn't what Mel expected. She wasn't sure what it was she *did* expect, but it wasn't this.

The huge—had to be bigger than a king—bed sat along one wall; the soft greens, blues, and yellows of the quilt definitely didn't scream "a male sleeps here". The bedding wasn't feminine but it wasn't masculine either, no heavy blacks or browns, and for a guy who appeared to be *all* guy, it struck her as odd.

Then again, who was she to say what fit Grady and what didn't?

She barely knew him. He'd shared a few childhood memories along with some adult ones, but she couldn't claim to *know* him.

Although, this tastefully decorated room—with its simple white furniture and what looked like family pictures framed on the walls, minus the usual bachelor accessory of big-screen TV or piles of dirty clothes—gave her more insight into who Grady was.

Either his mother had taught him well or he had a maid service.

Mel was leaning toward his mother's influence. From the stories Grady had shared, she guessed Mrs. Murdock wouldn't have sent her son out into the world without teaching him how to look after himself.

"We need to get you out of the rest of these clothes." Grady lowered her feet to the floor. He stripped his shirt over his head before starting on hers. Fingers fumbling, he muttered, "Stupid little buttons."

Mel grinned. "Here. Let me help." Starting at the bottom, she worked her way up until their hands met at her breasts.

She thought about drawing out the moment, about building anticipation, except he'd already seen her naked from the waist down. They'd already had sex. Taking her top off would be an anti-climax after what had just happened.

It was extremely gratifying to hear Grady suck in a fast breath when she parted her shirt to reveal the lacy demi bra she wore beneath.

"Jesus." His hands cupped her. His thumbs moved over the protruding peaks of her nipples, making her back arch and her insides quiver. "I knew you'd be gorgeous. But damn, woman. You steal my breath."

While he looked his fill, Mel looked hers. He was built; she knew that, had seen pictures, and his shorts and t-shirt had hinted at what lay underneath. But the sight of Grady without a stitch of clothing on...

Her gaze moved over his broad shoulders, down his pecs, lower to washboard abs, the deep valleys that ran along his hipbones, and finally to the part of him that was especially happy to see her.

Mel's eyes popped wide. For a split second she stayed

frozen in place before laughter tightened her belly and bubbled up her throat. He was fully erect and huge.

And still wore the used condom, the tip loaded with... well, his load.

She laughed harder. Bent forward, wrapping her arms around herself to hold her spasming sides.

Grady's hands went to his hips. "Not exactly the reaction I was anticipating."

Her funny bone had definitely been tickled and she couldn't stop laughing to get a word out. She barely managed to point at his groin.

Frowning, he looked down. "Shit." One large hand wrapped around his shaft. "Let me get rid of this." Turning, he headed through a doorway that gave a glimpse of white tile and chrome fittings.

She was still chuckling when he came back.

Grady's mouth kicked up on one end. "Now that the comic relief part of the evening is out of the way..."

Mel moved into his arms; slipping her own around his waist, she looked up. "I kinda like that you were so caught up in me you forgot." She smiled.

"Good thing."

"Oh?"

He bent his head, bringing his mouth down to hover over hers. "Yeah. 'Cause I'm not getting un-caught up in you anytime soon."

She didn't get a chance to reply. His mouth met hers, his lips firm and warm as they brushed back and forth. There was no diving in, only caress and retreat. It was a tantalizing lure that had her going up on her toes, pushing her naked body into his. Had her stroking her tongue over his lips until he opened for her.

Their tongues tangled but no matter how hard she tried to

speed things up, Grady wouldn't let her. A grumble of frustration rattled her throat.

Grady chuckled into her mouth. Pulling back, he looked down at her, his eyes black orbs with a rim of gold. "Slow this time."

"Slow's overrated." She latched her lips to his stubbled jaw. Sucked, then nibbled the hard curve before moving down his neck and exploring his chest.

His hand cupped the base of her skull, his fingers tangling in her hair. He used his hold to pull her head back. "Slow."

"But..." Mel lost her train of thought as Grady's other hand skimmed down her spine to her ass. Goose bumps rose behind the shiver that stole over her.

One of his hands cradled half her ass. Not half a cheek, half her ass. The man's hands were huge. Just like the rest of him, and when he squeezed the flesh in his hand she couldn't help the little moan of pleasure that slipped passed her lips.

"Slow," he murmured against her neck. "Slow so I can make sure I don't miss one inch of you."

Her head fell back on a louder, deeper moan when he used his mouth on the sensitive spot beneath her ear. He teased her lobe—flicked it with his tongue, sucked at it with his lips —and showed her why slow was as pleasurable as fast.

His hand continued to knead her ass cheek while the other stroked her body in leisurely sweeps of barely there caresses.

He explored her with his mouth and hands until she was ready to beg him for more.

She wanted him to toss her on the bed and have his way with her except the delicious slide of pleasure that was coursing through her proved too much to deny.

And for the first time in her life Mel let a man take charge.

CHAPTER 10

GRADY URGED Mel to take a step back. And another. He kept his lips and hands on her. Brushed and stroked over curves and dips. A flick of his wrist undid her bra, a sweep of his hands pushed the straps from her shoulders, and her last piece of clothing dropped to the floor at their feet.

He breathed her in. There were the lingering smells of her day but underneath it all was Mel. Sweet with a hot little kick. An enticing scent that had his mouth watering and his body tightening.

She drew him on so many levels, but this one—the tug of arousal deep in his bones—took precedence when he had her in his hands. Under his mouth.

Bending his knees, he lowered his head and sucked a hard nipple between his lips. He gripped it with his teeth, held it in place while he flicked with his tongue. She arched into him and he wrapped an arm around her back to keep her pinned against him.

"Grady." His name turned to a moan when he bit that puckered flesh harder.

Her fingernails dug into his shoulders and her hips rocked into him. She was trembling in his arms. Making sexy little sounds in the back of her throat.

A pulse of satisfaction thumped through him.

With every breath, she pulled at his control. Blood ran hot and fast in his veins, the pounding of his heart a drumbeat of passion that threatened to demolish his desire for slow.

"God. I can't get enough of you," he said around the tight bud in his mouth.

Opening his mouth wider, he sucked her in. Except the mouthful of breast didn't satisfy his hunger. He needed more. Needed on a level he'd never experienced. One that tore at his insides with razor-sharp edges.

With blinding clarity, he thought this must be how an addict felt. Gutted and euphoric in the same breath. Grady pulled his mouth from Mel and gasped, "More."

"Yes."

He picked her up. Carried her the last few feet to the bed and tossed her into the middle. She bounced once before he caged her in, pressing her deeper into the mattress with his body. "I know I said slow..." He flexed his hips.

She grinned at him. "And I said fast."

"Yeah. You did." He rocked into her. "Maybe we can do slow once I get my fill."

"Maybe." Mel parted her legs and his own slipped between, his cock nestling against the moist heat of her pussy. "Then again, fast was good."

Grady smiled down at her and ground his shaft along her clit. "Fast was definitely good."

Back and forth.

Mel shuddered. Gasped. "Condom."

"Top drawer." He tipped his chin to the left.

Together they reached for the handle and pulled the drawer out. Blindly, he rummaged around inside until he felt a foil square against his fingers.

She wiggled beneath him. The warm cushion of her pussy teased him, pressing at him in a wet kiss that drove him almost beyond reason. Surging to his knees, he tore open the packet and sheathed his throbbing cock.

He fell onto her. Finesse and civility were forgotten in his desperation to get inside her. Grabbing her knees, he pulled them out and pushed them back, spreading her wide open as he punched his hips forward and drove his length deep.

She bowed against him, her head thrown back. "Grady."

"Fuck."

For an instant, neither of them moved—half a second of time in which Grady savored the pure bliss of being inside Mel. He wasn't one for fanciful thoughts but in that brief moment, it seemed as though his whole life shifted. A tiny atom moved or rearranged or split open.

Whatever it was, nothing would ever be the same.

Mel bucked beneath him. She was pinned to the bed by his body but she still managed to rock her pelvis, her inner muscles gripping him in a slick clench that rippled along his shaft.

Heat and need and pleasure swamped him. Every nerve ending snapped to attention, as though he'd been struck by lightning. Jolted by the overwhelming sensations, all he could do was follow instinct.

Muscles and reflexes worked together, withdrawing and plunging his cock in and out of her tight pussy as he drove them both toward orgasm. He let go of her legs and she wrapped them around his waist, digging her heels into his ass as she surged up into him.

He powered in and out, his arms burrowed beneath her

back, his hands cupping her shoulders, holding her down, while he thrust hard and fast. Her fingers clawed at his back, her thighs tightening around him, as her words of encouragement filled his ears.

"More."

"Faster."

"Harder."

"Don't stop."

Sweat dripped from his forehead, coated his back and chest; the slick sound of their skin sticking together and pulling apart blended with the wet sounds of his cock forging in and out of her cream-soaked pussy.

His orgasm roared through him. The burst of heat erupted from his balls and washed over him with the force of a tidal wave. He had a split second to think of Mel before she was clamping down on him, her pussy squeezing the last of his come from his body as her walls convulsed around his shaft.

A strangled cry of pleasure spilled from her mouth as she sank her teeth into his shoulder.

Panting hard, Grady lowered his head to the pillow. Mel tucked her face in against his neck once her teeth let go. They lay gasping for breath, utterly spent.

"Holy fucking shit."

Grady snorted.

"No. Seriously, Grady." She leaned away to look at him. "Holy. Fucking. Shit."

"They *are* good words." He brushed her hair off her face. "And it's good to know the first time wasn't a fluke."

"Round one might not have been a fluke but this is definitely not normal." Her gaze darted away. "Well, not for me anyway."

He watched her chew the corner of her mouth and wondered at her hesitation. "Me either."

Her gaze came back to his. She licked her bottom lip and he bent his mouth to hers.

The kiss was meant to soothe—to reassure—but like everything about Mel, it proved too much for him to resist. He thrust his tongue into her mouth, coaxed hers out and sucked it, dragged his teeth over it. In seconds he was eating at her, his hips rocking into hers, blood once more rushing to his groin.

He pulled his mouth from hers. "Stay the night."

Grady tried to ignore the ripple of unease in his gut while she stared at him for long, breath-stalling seconds.

"Okay."

His chest deflated and he grinned. "Let's move things to the bathroom."

It looked like his two-person jacuzzi was finally going on its maiden voyage.

CHAPTER 11

THREE WEEKS LATER...

GRADY: This shit has to stop

Mel: I know. It'll get better. Promise.

Grady: When?

Mel: Next week. Friday?

Grady: That's five days away. Can't we swing something one night before that?

Mel: Can't. If I want Friday night off I need to work every night until then.

Grady: I'll take what I can get. Call me later?

Mel: After work? It'll be midnight before I get out of here.

Grady: Call me when you get home.

Mel: Don't you have training in the morning?

Grady: Call. Me.

Mel: Okay, okay, I'll call you.

Grady: Later.

. . .

GRADY TOSSED HIS PHONE ON THE COUCH BESIDE HIM AND sighed. He hadn't seen Mel in three weeks. Not since Monday morning after their one night together.

They'd each had to get to work and after some super hot morning sex followed by even hotter shower sex they'd gone their separate ways and not seen each other since.

They'd talked. And thank fuck for that. He'd have gone out of his mind if it weren't for those calls.

He scrubbed a hand down his face. He wanted to take Mel out for dinner—or lunch—but with both their schedules crazy busy, they hadn't managed it yet.

Good thing he wasn't a quitter. He'd keep trying until they managed to sync their calendars and he got more than just her voice in his ear.

Not that he objected to having her voice in his ear, he'd just prefer it to be because she was pressed up against him.

He smiled. The lack of face-to-face hadn't been a total loss. He'd learned more about Mel over the phone than if they'd been together because, let's be real, the two of them in a room meant clothes would be coming off and not a lot of talking would be done.

Resigned to eating alone again, he headed for the kitchen. Maybe he'd make a grilled cheese sandwich.

The motivation to cook was gone now that Mel wasn't coming over.

CHAPTER 12

FIVE DAYS LATER...

Mel wanted to scream but she didn't have the energy to puke—again—never mind yell.

Reaching for her phone she did what she'd hoped she wouldn't have to. Sent a text to Grady.

Mel: I have to cancel. Sorry.

Grady: Why?

Mel: I'm sick. That flu that was going round the office got me.

Grady: Do you need anything? Are you home?

Mel: I am. And I'm good. Just need to sleep it off.

Grady: I can come take care of you.

Mel: Oh, hell no. I'm not going to be responsible for taking Grade A off the field.

Grady: I'll wear a mask.

Mel: LOL Nope. I'll call when I'm sure you won't catch this thing.

Grady: Get better soon. Call if you need anything.

Mel: Thanks. Talk later.

DROPPING HER PHONE ON THE BED BESIDE HER, MEL rolled over and curled into a ball.

She couldn't afford to be sick. She'd had to take today off but she needed to be back on deck tomorrow.

Shaw Events was in charge of one of Miami's biggest charity events this weekend and she'd be damned if she let a little flu stop her from making it the most successful charity gala of the year.

She closed her eyes and wished she'd said yes to Grady coming over. She'd love to have his arms wrapped around her right now.

But she hadn't lied. There was no way she wanted to take him off the field, and this bug, whatever it was, had moved through her staff like wildfire this past week. He'd definitely catch it if he came near her.

Her stomach spasmed. There was no point moving, there was nothing left to bring up and she'd rather lie in bed dry retching than on the bathroom floor with her head over the toilet bowl.

Twenty-four hours.

That's how long everyone else had gone down with it.

She'd be fine by morning.

Then she could check her schedule and try to work out when she could fit in time with Grady.

Smiling, she fell asleep to thoughts of the man on every-one's minds since he'd pulled the Miami Storm to victory with some incredible moves.

CHAPTER 13

GRADY SAT SLOUCHED in the hard plastic chair and waited for Mel to pick up. He'd opted for a video call but he was rethinking that when he noticed a few heads turn his way.

Rummaging in his bag, he found his headphones and plugged them in just as Mel picked up.

Her smiling face filled his screen and her voice filled his ears.

"Hey! You won!"

He grinned. "We did."

"I'm not a football fan as a rule but that was one hell of a game there, Grade A."

He laughed, drawing more attention but he didn't care now he had Mel in front of him. His teammates had already worked out he was seeing someone. Or trying to anyway. "It was at that."

Mel's smile dimmed a bit. "You look tired."

"Exhausted. It'll be good to get home. If this plane ever takes off."

"I thought you weren't back until tomorrow."

"It will be tomorrow when we land."

"Ah, okay, well, once you get in and catch some sleep, message me and we'll attempt to match up our schedules."

"Oh, you can bet that sweet ass of yours we'll be doing that."

It had been four and a half weeks since they'd met. Four and a half weeks since he'd touched her, kissed her.

Phone calls and video chats just weren't cutting it. He'd be seeing her in the flesh this week if he had to hunt her down at work.

She chewed her bottom lip then blurted, "Maybe this is the universe's way of telling us we shouldn't see each other."

"Bullshit. It's two busy people working out the best way to fit together."

He wasn't letting her back out of this. They'd spent less than twenty-four hours together over four weeks ago and he knew without a doubt he wanted more time with this woman.

"We'll work it out."

They had to. The other option wasn't acceptable.

The airport PA system crackled before a man announced the plane was ready to board. "I've got to go. It'll be too late when I get in so I'll call you tomorrow. Okay?"

Mel sighed. "Yeah. Safe travels."

She disconnected before he could say anything else.

CHAPTER 14
FOUR DAYS LATER...

GRADY GRABBED the bag off his passenger seat and grinned.

He was finally, *finally* going to get to see Mel.

They couldn't sync up their calendars this week due to all the events Mel's company was running but she was in the office today and when she'd told him she'd be working through lunch, he'd decided to surprise her by bringing her something better than the PB&J sandwich she had packed.

Shaw Events was located in a strip mall that wasn't high end or rundown. When he scanned the other businesses, he saw a lawyer, a doctor, a dentist, a dress shop, and what looked like a furniture store.

The products in the windows of the last two looked expensive and the streets he'd driven down told him this was an affluent area of the city.

He'd never been in this part of town before. He could see the appeal though. It was a nice middle-class suburb and when he thought about it, the area suited Mel. She was classy without the flash or pomp.

And he knew she'd grown up without parents and been

raised by her grandparents who didn't have an abundance of money, but they hadn't been poor.

She'd told him the money she'd inherited when they died had paid off her student loans and given her the ability to start her own company.

She had a solid work ethic and unlike some of the women who hung around professional athletes, she didn't expect a handout.

In fact she'd probably insist on paying for her own lunch.

Smiling, he pulled open the door that read in stylized gold script 'Shaw Events' and stepped into the cool air-conditioned office.

"Hi, can I help you?" the girl behind the reception desk asked.

"Yep. I'm here to see Melinda Shaw." He figured he'd keep things professional and use her full name. They hadn't talked about whether or not she'd told people they were dating. Not that they'd been out on a date. Yet.

"Oh." She glanced down at her desk. "There isn't an appointment on her calendar..."

"It's a last-minute thing." He held up the bag in his hand. "We're working through lunch."

She frowned but reached for the phone. "Who should I say is here?"

"Grady Murdock."

The girl's eyes bugged out. "Oh gosh. You're—"

"Grady?"

He turned to see Mel standing in a doorway at the back of the room. "Hey."

"What—?"

"I brought lunch." He moved toward her, noticing most of the desks in this area were empty. "Couldn't have you working through lunch with only a PB&J." He grinned.

"Is that..." She drew in a deep breath. "Oh my god, if that's what I think it is, I'm going to owe you big."

Grady's grin widened. "You owe me."

"Give me that." She reached for the bag but he held it up high.

"There's enough for two in here." He tipped his chin toward the door behind her. "Invite me in."

"You're holding my favorite meal in that bag, Grady; you don't need an invitation." Turning on her heel, she led the way into her office, giving him a view of her gorgeous ass.

He closed the door behind them and looked around. The space was clean, simple. Some filing cabinets, a desk with two chairs in front and a small glass-doored refrigerator filled with bottles of water. "Nice office."

"Thanks. Let me clear the desk off, then we can eat." She began piling files and moving them to the floor beside the desk. "I can't believe you remembered not only my favorite meal but the restaurant too."

"I hope it's not too cold. It's clear on the other side of town. I should have bought a thermal bag or something." He didn't care if he ate a cold meal—he'd done that plenty of times in college, but he wanted Mel to enjoy this meal and their time together.

"Grady."

He absently said, "Yeah," while pulling out the two takeout contains filled with moussaka, and the plastic cutlery they'd given him when he'd picked up the order.

She placed a hand on his arm, stopping him from what he was doing.

Glancing up he found her eyes glistening. "Hey." He let go of their lunch and pulled her into a hug. "What's wrong?"

"Thank you." She sounded choked up.

"Thank you?" What the hell?

"For lunch. The PB&J was as much as I could manage this morning and I ate that three hours ago," she mumbled into his chest. "I swear, I'm running on empty these days. Ever since I had that flu."

"What you are is overworked." He should know; they'd been unable to connect for weeks because of how busy she was. How hard she worked. "I'm not telling you how to run your business but do you have enough staff?" The thought had crossed his mind more than once.

She pushed out of his arms. "Yes, but we've had back-to-back events, sometimes two on one day, for weeks now and with this flu sweeping through the office—twice—we've been playing catch up a lot."

"Well. Sit down. Take thirty minutes to eat lunch with me and hopefully you'll have more energy when we're done."

Pushing up onto her toes, she kissed his cheek. "Thank you."

He smiled. "You're more than welcome."

They took the seats in front of her desk and neither of them talked while they devoured the delicious Greek cuisine.

He'd never had moussaka before but he had to admit he could see why Mel loved it. He would have to see about trying his hand at making it.

It was basically lasagna with eggplant and he made a mean lasagna even if he said so himself.

Mel dropped her fork into the empty takeout container and sighed. "God, that hit the spot."

She'd shoveled it in quicker than him. He still had a third left. "Want the rest of mine?" he offered.

She eyed him sideways. "I shouldn't..."

Before he could argue why she should, she'd yanked the container from his hands and taken a bite.

Smiling, he watched her devour the rest of his lunch. He'd

grab something else on the way home. That had been his plan anyway.

He'd had to increase his calorie intake since the season had started and he'd known when he'd picked up their order, it wouldn't be enough to fill him.

"Mel—" a woman burst into the room behind them. "Oh, sorry."

"It's all right, Carla. What's up?"

"The Mackinaw event."

"What is Mrs. Mackinaw objecting to now?" Mel asked with a sigh.

"She wants more male servers than female. In fact she'd prefer no females serve the guests. She doesn't object to them being in the kitchen but she doesn't want them around the guests."

Mel brought a hand to her face and pinched the bridge of her nose. "Let me guess. She doesn't want anything to distract from her precious Belle."

"She didn't say that exactly but yes, that's my take."

"Okay. Give me five and we'll see if we can swing it." Mel looked at him. "I'm sorry."

"No problem." Grady was disappointed but he understood. He got to his feet and began clearing up their mess.

"Leave that. I'll deal with it."

"Nope. You deal with enough. I'll take care of this because I can." He nodded at the other woman. "You take care of that because you can."

She smiled at him. "I'm not sure why—"

"Don't." He pressed a finger to her mouth. "You know why."

Her gaze searched his and he wasn't sure what she saw there but she nodded once and smiled. "I'll call you later," she said against his finger.

"Anytime." He dropped a kiss on her lips and left because if he lingered he'd want a longer kiss which would lead to wanting to get her naked, and that wasn't going to happen now.

And the fantasies he'd had about bending her over her desk were definitely out of the question.

He dumped their trash in a bin outside when he hit the street. They might not have gotten that much time together but he was more than happy with today's lunch date.

It might be proving difficult to sync their schedules, but as far as he was concerned it was worth it.

CHAPTER 15

TWO WEEKS LATER...

"Jesus. You look like shit."

Mel raised her head from the desk and found Carla hovering just inside her office door. Closing her eyes, she lowered her head back down and wished her assistant away.

"No. Seriously, Mel, you need to go see a doctor or something."

"Hmm." The hum was all she could manage in reply.

"How long is it now?" Carla's voice sounded right in Mel's ear, almost burst her eardrum.

She groaned as a wave of nausea rushed up her throat. With a twist of her upper body—something she'd become extremely proficient at of late—Mel had her face over the waste bin next to her desk and proceeded to dry heave in a futile attempt to empty her stomach.

That sucker had been evacuated long ago. Right now, her internal organs were holding on for dear life in case her malevolent stomach came after them next.

"It has to be more than a stomach flu. You've been sick on

and off for weeks." Carla's hand smoothed up and down Mel's back.

"No time,"—her torso contracted, her belly button practically hitting her spine—"to be sick."

"No one has time to be sick but if you don't accept that you are, and rest, you'll never get better."

Mel knew her assistant meant well. She also knew Carla was right. And after today, she'd have three days to lie in bed and die a quiet, easy—or not—death.

Confident the purging had stopped for now, Mel sat up and leaned back in her chair. "I'm going home to bed this afternoon and staying there until Friday."

Carla sucked in a breath. "Jesus. You really *do* look like shit."

She eyed her frowning assistant. She'd dropped a few pounds since she'd gotten sick the first time and the sunken, dark half-circles under her eyes made her look worse, but Mel had thought she'd covered both of those up with makeup and clothes.

"Go home. You don't need to be here. I can take care of everything."

Carla was capable but Mel had a hard time handing over the reins of her baby. She'd gone from a two-man—or in their case, woman—show to a twenty-five-strong operation, with another forty or so casual employees.

Still, Carla had been the other half of the two, and she knew Shaw Events back to front.

Sighing, Mel shut her eyes. "Fine. I'll go. On the condition you call if you need me."

Carla laughed. "Sure thing, boss."

Frowning, Mel cracked open one eye. "I detect sarcasm."

"Never." Carla attempted a straight face.

For what felt like the first time in days, Mel smiled.

"C'mon. Let's get you in a cab."

"Don't need a cab. I drove to work." Not that Mel remembered the drive in. She yawned. It was hours ago—wasn't it? She was so exhausted lately that days blurred together.

"And that's what worries me. You can barely stand and you got behind the wheel of a car." Carla picked up Mel's briefcase —the one she hadn't unpacked—and slung it over a shoulder before gripping Mel's arm and helping her out of the chair. "How about Davie drives you home then gets a cab back? Will that make you happy?"

Mel nodded, causing her head to spin and her stomach to churn. "Yes," she muttered, worried she was about to have another bout of retching.

"Good, that'll work for me too."

Davie was their fifty-six-year-old administrative assistant. Or more accurately, their admin genius. There wasn't anything the man couldn't do or make happen. Mel was more than happy to put herself in his capable hands.

"She finally giving up?" Davie asked as they entered the outer office.

"Yes. Can you drive her home and grab a cab back?" Carla asked while Mel wobbled on her feet, putting a hand on Davie's desk to keep herself upright.

If she didn't stop throwing up everything she ate soon, she'd find herself too weak to stand even with the help of a desk and her assistant.

"Of course." A thick arm slid around her waist as Davie's voice boomed in her ear. "Let's get you home and into bed."

He probably wasn't yelling but everything seemed magnified. His arm around her hurt and the sounds and voices of the busy office were eardrum-splitting decibels.

Mel groaned and leaned away from Davie. "Don't get close. Don't want to pass this on."

Davie laughed. The sound vibrated through her, rattling bones and bouncing her brain around her skull like a pinball pinging off bumpers. "I'm made of tougher stuff than that. Besides, you've had this thing for weeks and no one else has come down with it this bad."

It was true. Normally a bug like this passed through the office like a wildfire through a dry grass field and then it was gone.

Maybe she had food poisoning?

But that didn't make any sense. And right now her fuzzy brain didn't have the ability to work out what was going on. She barely had the power to function.

Although she wasn't doing a bang up job of that, considering she tripped over her own feet.

"Whoa." Davie's arm tightened. "I've got you."

The world spun as Davie swung her off her feet and into his arms. For an old guy, he was in good shape. From there, things got blurry. She dozed off in the car and only came awake when they'd reached her house and Davie was easing her out of the passenger seat and into his arms.

"I can walk," she protested. Admittedly it was weak, and in opposition to the way she wrapped her arms around his neck and held on, her head resting on his shoulder.

"You need to see your doctor." He managed to get her house key in the lock and the door open without putting her down. "This isn't a normal flu. The only time I've seen someone this sick was when Daisy was pregnant with our Shelly."

The word 'pregnant' stuck in her head, but Mel shook it loose and attempted to get control of her spinning thoughts. "Just put me on the couch. I'll be fine now that I'm home."

"You're sure?" Davie lowered her to the L-shaped

sectional that took up most of her living room. "You ring me or Carla if you need anything."

"I will." Mel managed a half smile. "Promise."

It took a few more minutes of reassuring him she'd call if she needed anything but finally Davie left and she was alone.

She slumped back against the couch and let the exhaustion take her under.

CHAPTER 16

GRADY CHECKED his phone once more and frowned before shoving it in his bag. Mel hadn't returned any of his calls.

In the weeks since they'd met, he'd managed one meal—lunch he'd taken to her office—and numerous phone calls and video chats with the woman.

She was busy. He got that. He was busy too.

Preseason and now the regular season had him in and out of Miami. Except he'd thought they'd fit in more time together than they had.

He'd barely succeeded in convincing her to see him after their one night together. He smiled remembering the way he'd gotten around her no-time-to-see-anyone declaration. His argument had been twisted but successful.

"You're not seeing anyone. I'm not seeing anyone. We should not see anyone together."

She'd laughed until she realized he was serious. For a second Grady had thought he'd have to do a little more cajoling, but she'd pulled out her iPad and opened her calendar, finding a date they were both free the next week.

That one had to be canceled. And the one after that too. And the one after that...

He'd finally gotten to see her by taking lunch to her office.

That was two weeks ago.

Not that they hadn't burned up the cell network and Internet. Texts. Calls. Video calls. They'd fired back and forth all day, every day, until three days ago.

He knew she'd been sick—again—for over a week this time and now he was really worried.

She didn't have any close family and her best friend lived in New York, so who was looking after her? Who was making sure she was eating and drinking and seeing a doctor if that was what she needed?

"Yo. Grade A?" Garrett yelled from the locker-room door. "You coming?"

Grady shook himself. Cleared his mind as he grabbed his helmet. He had a game to play, and if he didn't get his head in it, he risked fucking up on the field.

A hand clapped his shoulder and he turned to see Jax Elliot standing next to him. "Whatever it is, clear it out. Focus on the ball and what you have to do with it," Jax said.

"How'd you know?"

"I've seen that look a time or two in the mirror." Jax slapped Grady's shoulder twice more then moved toward the door.

He glanced at his bag before pulling in a deep breath. The smell of the room—sweat mingled with the scent of liniment, and the unmistakable odor of a bunch of guys in close quarters—did what the pep-talk from Jax and Grady's own attempts to rid himself of outside worries couldn't.

It focused him. Got his head in the game and his muscles relaxing in a way only football ever did.

And sex with Mel.

His body tightened.

"Shit." He shook his head. "Now isn't the time."

As soon as the game was over tonight, he'd track her down and make sure she was okay.

And if she wasn't, he'd do whatever it took to make her better.

He joined the rest of the team in the tunnel and waited to enter the stadium. The roar of the crowd vibrated through the concrete under his feet.

Grinning, he followed his teammates, jogging out onto the field to the thundering applause of the Storm's dedicated fans.

This—the unwavering support of the fans—was a close second to why Grady loved football. First was that euphoric rush that fizzed in his blood when he took the ball into the end zone.

He'd scored in every game so far this season and he wasn't about to break that streak. Especially in the first home game of the regular season.

It was an even split so far, two away preseason games and two at home. Last week they'd been in New York against the Dragons for the regular season kickoff.

Tonight they were home against the New Orleans Tigers, and Grady planned to win.

By the time the whistle blew at the end of the third quarter, it wasn't looking as though Grady would keep his scoring streak—or the Storm would leave the field victors.

As a team, they knuckled down, got over the line and kept the opposition scoreless, and with two minutes left on the clock in the fourth, the Storm took possession of the ball.

Expectation hung heavy in the air. Everyone knew this was it. They were four points down and if ever they needed to pull out a miracle touchdown, it was now.

They took position and a hush fell over the arena. Grady

couldn't say what happen next; his eyes were glued to the end of the field and the zone.

Storm's center snapped the ball and Grady took off. He knew the play, could run it in his sleep; he just had to run it through the Tigers defense.

In a corner of his mind, he felt the burn as he pumped his legs, dodged and weaved his way down the field, the sideline on his right.

A couple of yards from the end zone he darted left, tipped his head in the same direction and saw the ball bulleting his way.

It was high.

In a split second, Grady launched into the air and barely got his hand on the ball. He pulled it in, hit the ground, and took the last two steps into the zone.

Touchdown.

The crowd erupted in the stands and his teammates surrounded him. They slapped his back, his helmet, his ass.

He smiled through the rest of the game. They kicked for a PAT then played it safe, keeping the Tigers from scoring and left the field with a three-point winning margin.

The celebrations followed them into the locker room. The president and managers came down to congratulate the team, each of them finding their way over to praise him personally.

Grady took the compliments and gratitude with the expected good grace, all the while making sure to point out he couldn't have made the play without his team.

Storm's president Mark Mitchum came over last.

"Great catch." Mark held out a hand.

Shaking hands, Grady answered, "Thanks. It was a great win for the team."

Mark smiled. "Yes, it was. You up for a quick interview?"

Grady knew interviews were part of the job but it didn't mean he had to like them. Still, he wasn't about to say no to the boss. "Sure."

It only took a few minutes to answer a couple of questions. Once that was dealt with, Grady snuck away to shower. He needed to get going.

If he didn't leave soon, it would be too late to call Mel—or stop by her house if she didn't answer her phone.

CHAPTER 17

Mel woke with a start.

Her neck, bent at a weird angle, hurt like hell when she moved. It took her a moment to remember where she was.

Home.

She glanced around. On her couch. In the dark. She must have slept for hours.

Her nausea had subsided a little, which it did most evenings. It didn't fail to get her hopes up, like it had every other day since she'd become sick again.

Pushing to her feet, she took a few cautious steps toward the bedroom. Confident she wasn't about to collapse, she kept going.

Approaching the small table in the hallway, she noticed her answering-machine light blinking. She hit the play button on the way past but stopped the second Sadie's voice came through the speaker.

"Hey, you. Haven't heard from you in days. Hope you're over the flu by now. Me, on the other hand...I'm not likely to stop feeling sick for weeks. Morning sickness has to be ten times worse than any stomach flu. Day and night. Anyway, call me. I miss our nightly chats."

Morning sickness...

Davie's words rolled through her head.

"This isn't a normal flu. The only time I've seen someone this sick was when Daisy was pregnant with our Shelly."

"No." She was on the pill and they'd used condoms.

She was on the pill!

They'd used condoms!

"This cannot be happening."

Moving quicker than she had in recent days, Mel rushed to her bathroom and yanked open the top drawer.

She checked the packet, knew she'd finished one about a week ago, remembered getting the new script the day after she'd spent the night with Grady.

That was seven weeks ago.

And she hadn't had a period.

"Oh God." Bile rose in her throat and she swallowed it back. Her hand shook as she replaced the packet and closed the drawer. "I need to take a test."

She headed back to the living room for her purse and keys. There was an all-night pharmacy five minutes away. It was where she filled her contraceptive prescription.

She'd pick up one of those home pregnancy tests and put her mind at ease within the hour.

The humid night engulfed her when she stepped outside. Getting in her car, she started it and waited for the AC to cool the interior before pulling out of her driveway.

She drove with care, mindful of her weakness and slower reflexes. She probably shouldn't be driving at all, but there was no way she was waiting any longer to discover if what she was suffering from wasn't an *illness*—like she was beginning to suspect.

Parking in a spot by the door, Mel was out of the car and inside the Walgreens scanning the aisles for pregnancy tests in less than a minute.

When she found them, she stared at the numerous choices.

"Why are there so many? Surely I don't need this many options?" She started at the top shelf and read the back of every box before she decided on which to purchase.

The box held three tests. She liked the idea of having the opportunity to take it a second time to be sure of the correct result. "Best out of three." Mel giggled.

Shit. Why was she laughing? This wasn't funny.

"Can I help you?"

"Oh." She spun toward the woman wearing a shirt with the store logo over her left breast, a nametag on the right. "No. I'm fine, thanks." Mel held up her chosen box.

"That's our best-selling brand," May—according to her nametag—said.

She smiled at the woman. "Good to know."

"Hope the answer's the one you want."

Mel wasn't sure if it was her disheveled state or the deer-caught-in-headlights look she must have, but she had the impression the woman knew this wasn't a planned event. If it even *was* an event.

"Thank you."

"I'll ring you up." May took the box from Mel's hand and led the way to the checkout.

She swiped her debit card and punched in her pin when asked. Transaction approved, she took the paper bag May held out. "Thanks again."

"You're welcome. Have a good evening."

Leaving the store and climbing back into her car, Mel

took a deep breath and realized there was no way she could go home and do this alone.

In spite of their not-really-a-relationship relationship, if this test proved positive, she wanted Grady with her when she found out.

Hell. She wanted him with her even if it was a false alarm.

She knew he was in town, that he had a home game tonight, and glancing at the clock, she figured he'd be on the field now. She had time to go home and change out of her work clothes, shower. Try to eat something. The thought of food made her stomach roll.

The drive home didn't go as well as the drive to Walgreens. She felt nauseous and shaky and sweaty and her eyes kept closing. And if one more yawn cracked her jaw, the damn thing would dislocate.

Pulling into her drive what felt like a billion years later, she switched off the car and lowered her head to the wheel.

Several deep breaths later, she roused herself enough to get out of the car and into the house. She dumped her purse, keys, and Walgreens bag on the floor by the front door and headed straight for the bathroom, where she stripped out of her clothes and stepped into the shower.

She turned on the water and sank to the floor. Warm spray rained down on her and, tilting her head back, Mel let it wash over her face.

The stream soothed her, even woke her up a little, but there was no ignoring the fatigue that had overtaken her.

She'd never felt so drained of energy.

Even washing herself was proving difficult. The soap was out of reach and she couldn't seem to work up the slightest bit of concern that lying in the bottom of her shower wouldn't get the job done properly.

It wasn't until the water ran cold that she found the gumption to turn the shower off, and only because she started to shiver and knew staying where she was definitely *would* make her sick.

A few swipes of a towel were sufficient to dry her so she didn't drip on the floor. Still damp, she went into her bedroom and found her most comfy clothes.

Sweatpants—cut above the knee—and an old college football jersey she'd swiped from some guy she'd dated way back when. She didn't bother with underwear.

Slipping her feet into a pair of flip-flops, she made her way to her phone and called an Uber.

She wouldn't risk driving again tonight and she really wanted to see Grady.

The sudden need for him scared her. As much as the thought of being pregnant did.

She hadn't relied on anyone since leaving home for college. And she'd never looked back.

Sadie was the closest thing to family Mel had, and they'd spent the last four years in separate parts of the country. Their friendship remained strong but Sadie had Alex now— and a baby on the way.

That thought stopped her. She smoothed a hand over her flat stomach. "Oh God. What if I'm pregnant too?"

She'd cross that bridge when she came to it. Like every other hurdle in her life, she'd deal with it as best she could. And if she didn't have a clue how to do that, she'd fake it 'til she made it.

Except if this was happening, she wasn't doing it on her own—*hadn't* done it on her own.

Grabbing her purse, keys, and the bag holding the pregnancy test, she slipped out the front door and waited for the Uber to arrive.

CHAPTER 18

GRADY PULLED INTO THE DRIVEWAY, his headlights flashing over something piled on his porch. Hitting the remote to open the garage door, he parked and climbed out.

Instead of going inside through the connecting door, he headed back out into the night.

As he got closer to his front door, he realized the pile was actually a person. "Mel?"

She didn't stir.

Panic exploded in his gut and he sprinted the last few feet, dropping to his knees beside her.

"Jesus. Mel?" He gave her a little shake.

"Mmm."

"What are you doing out here?" He helped her sit up.

"Not home."

Grady brushed the hair out of her face and noticed dark bruises beneath her eyes. "Are you still sick?"

"Hmm...'bout that."

"C'mon." He scooped her into his arms and stood. "Let's get you inside."

Instead of bothering with keys, he headed back to the garage and through the connecting door. He'd get her settled in bed then come back and lock up.

She snuggled into his chest and Grady's body responded. Ruthlessly he squashed down the surge of lust and concentrated on taking care of Mel.

She'd gone back to sleep by the time he lowered her to his bed. Tucking her in, he dropped a kiss on her forehead. "Back in a sec."

It took him longer than a second but no more than two minutes to lock up and return to her side.

She hadn't moved.

Curled up on her side facing the door, the covers tucked beneath her chin, Grady couldn't help wishing he came home to this sight every night.

She obviously needed sleep and he was wiped out from tonight's game, so he shucked his clothes and crawled into bed behind her.

Wrapping an arm around her waist, he pulled her back against him.

The only problem with the situation was Mel's current state of dress. The problem being she *was* dressed. She'd be more comfortable without clothes but he wasn't about to strip her. He wasn't that presumptuous or stupid.

Smiling, he buried his face in her hair and breathed deep.

God, he'd missed the smell of her.

She'd recently showered; the scent of water and her damp hair were obvious indicators.

He ran a hand over her side, his fingers bumping over each rib.

He didn't remember her being this thin last time he'd touched her.

The stomach flu she'd picked up a few weeks ago and then again this past week had really done a number on her.

She'd lost weight, and those bruised eyes only highlighted the gauntness of her face.

She needed some TLC, and he was just the man to deliver it.

He yawned.

First thing in the morning. After they'd both had a good night's sleep.

Sometime later, Grady woke with a grunt. The result of an elbow to the gut. Mel scrambled out of bed and ran for the bathroom. She'd only made it halfway across the bedroom when he heard her retching.

Throwing back the covers, Grady followed. When he entered the bathroom, he found her on the floor, head leaning over the toilet, body jerking with each convulsion as she emptied her stomach.

He grabbed a facecloth and ran it under the cold water. Moving next to her, he crouched down, brushed her hair aside, and placed the cool towel on the back of her neck.

Each jolt of her body made him cringe. The only thing he could do was keep her hair out of the way and wait for the vomiting spell to pass.

When she finally lifted her head, tears ran down her face and a stream of dribble dangled from her mouth.

Using the wet cloth, he wiped her mouth and helped her off the floor. She was shaking and slick with sweat, and he quickly stripped her out of her pants and top and stepped them both into the shower.

"Have you seen a doctor?" Grady turned the tap on. "You were sick weeks ago and again now. It can't be your average stomach bug you've caught."

"Don't think I'm sick," she murmured into his chest.

He chuckled. "Oh, that was definitely sick."

"Pregnant."

Grady stilled. "What?"

She leaned back but stayed in his arms. Her eyes were glassy, her forehead furrowed. "I think I'm pregnant."

"You think?" Jesus. *Pregnant?*

"I bought a test."

"What did it say?"

"Haven't done it yet."

"Where is it? We'll do it now."

"I brought it with me…" She glanced around them.

"I didn't see anything when I picked you up out front but the light wasn't on."

"I had my purse and keys too."

"Okay, give me a second."

Grady leaned her against the shower wall, waited until she was steady before letting go.

"I'll go look on the porch."

He snagged a towel and wrapped it around his hips as he walked through the house dripping water on the floor.

Flicking on the outside light, he opened the front door and immediately spotted her purse and keys beside a Walgreens bag.

With her things in hand, he locked up again and headed back to the bathroom.

"All right. Let's see what we have to do." He helped Mel out of the shower and sat her on the side of the tub, a towel around her shoulders.

"I think I have to pee in a cup or on the stick or something."

Grady scanned the directions and got everything ready. "Okay. On the stick or in a cup?"

"Peeing on it would be less messy." She shrugged. "No cleanup."

He handed over the test stick. "When you're ready, take the cap off and put it in..." He consulted the instructions again to make sure he had it right. "Midstream for five seconds. Then we wait about three minutes for the result."

Mel managed a half-smile as she rose to her feet. "Thanks."

"What for? Knocking you up?"

"We don't know that yet."

Grady moved to the door. "If you were at all unsure, you wouldn't be here." He closed the door between them.

He didn't understand why he was so calm. He should be freaking out. He'd never pictured himself in this position. He'd always been careful. *They'd* been careful. But if she was pregnant, they'd deal with it.

Together.

And the fact that the idea of Mel being pregnant with his baby sent a thrill of happiness through him told Grady why he wasn't freaking out.

On some level, he wanted this with her.

CHAPTER 19

Mel stared at the stick on the counter. Two pink lines. What did that mean? She was pregnant twice?

"First thing tomorrow, we'll organize whatever paperwork we need to get married," Grady said beside her.

Her mouth dropped open as she turned to face him.

"We need to find a doctor too."

She gaped at him and he kept right on talking.

"And get you moved in here."

Was he insane? "We're not getting married."

"Of course we are."

She shook her head, gripping the counter when her head spun. "No. We're not. And I'm not moving in with you, either."

"But we're having a baby."

Oh God, we're having a baby!

Mel took a shuddering breath. She would not freak out. Would not. "That's no reason to get married or move in together."

"But what about the baby?" He seemed genuinely puzzled by her refusal.

"What about it?"

"It's mine."

"No question."

"Then why won't you let me do the right thing?"

"Grady, this isn't the Dark Ages where the knocked-up woman is forced to marry the guy who knocked her up. Taking responsibility and being involved in the child's life is doing the right thing."

She lowered herself to the edge of the bath. She was feeling a little more lightheaded than normal now that they knew for sure she was pregnant.

How the hell had she ended up impregnated when they'd used *two* different kinds of contraception?

He must have super-sperm.

A giggle slipped free and Grady scowled down at her.

"What's funny?"

"Super-sperm."

"What?"

"You must have super-sperm. We used condoms—"

"They're not one-hundred—"

"And I'm on the pill."

"Oh." He frowned.

"Yeah. Super-sperm."

He grinned. "Super-sperm, huh?"

She shook her head and a wave of dizziness quickly followed by a surge of nausea sent her lunging for the toilet once more.

God, would this morning sickness ever stop?

"Here." Grady gathered her hair and twisted it on top of her head, holding it there with one hand while pressing a cool cloth to the base of her neck with the other. "Definitely need to see a doctor ASAP. This can't be normal, and even I can see you've lost weight. I thought you were supposed to put it *on* when you're pregnant."

Her stomach spasmed, knotting tighter and tighter with each contraction because there was nothing left inside her to bring up. She groaned and leaned into Grady.

"How often are you sick?" he asked as he massaged her neck.

"Comes and goes, but generally it's been all day, every day."

"Why didn't you tell me you were this bad?"

She took a deep breath as this round of nausea eased. "Thought it was the flu hanging on. Know different now."

"C'mon, let's get you back in bed." Effortlessly he picked her up and carried her into the bedroom.

"What about when I'm sick again?"

"I'll get a bucket." Grady placed her gently on the bed, took the towel from around her, and pulled the covers up to her chin. "I'll get you some water. You need to keep up your fluids even though your body is rejecting everything."

"I know." Mel smiled as Grady left the room.

It had been so long since anyone had taken care of her. She'd forgotten how nice it felt. Her eyelids drifted shut.

God, she was tired.

"Mel." Grady ran his fingers through her damp hair and cupped the back of her head. "Sit up and take a sip of this for me."

It was easy to do with his help. The cold water soothed her raw throat and for now, sat in her belly without bouncing back out.

"Not so fast." He took the glass away and put it on the bedside table. "Too much will make your stomach revolt again."

She lay back and let him tuck her in. "Thank you," she murmured.

"Try to get some sleep."

"All I seem to do is sleep or throw up."

"We'll sort that out tomorrow."

Her mind was fuzzy. She didn't have any idea how they'd sort it out. The nausea wouldn't go away unless she wasn't pregnant...

"Grady?"

"Yeah." He was sliding into bed behind her.

"I'm keeping the baby."

He drew in a quick breath.

"I'm not getting rid of it."

"God! Mel." He pulled her back against his chest, his forehead resting on her shoulder. "I don't want that. I'd never ask you to do that."

She sighed. "Okay."

"Mel."

"Hmm...?"

"This might not be planned but I don't regret it. Not for a second."

Not yet he didn't. They hadn't really faced the reality of the situation, though. He'd proposed marriage and moving in together. She was too sick to think about any of that except to know she couldn't agree.

They weren't even dating. They'd had sex once.

Fine. More than once, but it had only been one night.

Since then they'd spent numerous hours texting, calling, video chatting, any way they could find to connect.

All their talking had built a tentative friendship, the start of a relationship that might have gotten to this point eventually—in a couple of years maybe.

Or it might have burned bright and fizzled out within a few months.

But when she looked at everything that had happened between them, they'd basically gotten pregnant from a one-night stand.

CHAPTER 20

GRADY HELD Mel until she dropped into a deep sleep.

Careful not to wake her, he untangled himself and slid out of bed. He made sure she was covered before pulling on a pair of boxers and heading for his home office.

Grabbing his laptop and phone, he detoured past the kitchen for a bottle of water and the bucket he'd forgotten to grab earlier, then returned to the bedroom.

Settling on the bed, he booted up his computer. He needed to do some research. He wanted to have a plan before she woke and began arguing with him.

But where did he start?

He'd never considered being a father except in a far-off-in-the-distant-future way. A wife and family had definitely been on the horizon, but that's as close as they'd ever come in his mind. He glanced at Mel.

Now he had both.

Well, maybe not the wife. Yet.

As cliché as it sounded, he'd known there was something different about Mel from the moment he'd bumped into her.

Of course, it never entered his mind she'd be the mother of his child.

Their night together had blown his mind, and while he'd love a repeat, he wanted more than just sex with her.

He'd proven that, hadn't he? With the constant calling and texting? They'd even spent a memorable morning—and two a.m. was as morning as it got—on a video chat.

He smiled, recalling the way she'd blushed at his suggestion they have phone sex with visuals.

They'd gotten to know each other in a way they probably wouldn't have if they'd dated normally. By not seeing each other in person, they'd been forced to talk.

She was funny and smart and independent. She'd built her business from the ground up with a dedication that showed in her success.

He admired her. Respected her. *Liked* her.

If he was going to be thrown into parenting headfirst with anyone, he'd want it to be with Mel.

Good thing, considering...

She stirred. Murmured something unintelligible and rolled over, curling herself against his side. He lifted the laptop out of the way as she slid her arm over his legs and snuggled her face into his hip.

Wiggling until she was comfortable, she finally ended up with her head in his lap and an arm and leg thrown over him, as though she were trying to pin him in place.

He smiled. He wasn't going anywhere. And if her unconscious actions were an indication, neither was she.

He put the laptop on the floor beside the bed without unsettling her. Running his fingers through her hair, he leaned his head back on the headboard and closed his eyes.

He'd wait a few minutes then move her off him so he

could get back to looking up all he could find about pregnancy and how to get married.

Grady grinned.

The idea of Mel being tied to him made him happy. But he wasn't an idiot. He knew neither of them would have chosen this—not right now.

Their chemistry was instant and explosive, it burned flash-fire hot, and while he knew that wasn't a guaranteed happy-ever-after, he didn't think what they had was going to burn out anytime soon.

He'd like to believe he was experienced enough to know the difference between pure physical attraction and a deeper connection.

They had the deeper kind. He just had to convince Mel of that. And that wouldn't happen without some facts. Or without a lot of effort on his part to show her he was serious about them as a couple.

As gently as he could, Grady lifted her off his lap. Dead to the world, she moved without protest, and he was able to guide her onto her pillow and tuck the covers around her without any trouble.

Not wanting to risk disturbing her again, he picked up his laptop and moved to the window seat his mother had insisted was a selling point of the house.

He smiled, thinking about how happy his parents would be when they found out they were going to be grandparents.

Lord knows they'd never pressured him or his siblings to become parents but they'd made it perfectly clear they were ready whenever grandkids arrived.

They'd be thrilled when he told them.

He frowned. He couldn't tell them yet.

Not until everything was straightened out between him

and Mel. It might even be best to wait until she was feeling better.

When would that be…?

Typing the words "what to expect when you're pregnant" into a search engine, he waited for links to pop up.

He opened the first five in new tabs and started reading.

Within ten minutes his eyes crossed and his mind boggled.

There were books they should purchase to have on hand. Vitamins Mel needed to take. Classes they should attend. Doctor's appointments. Hospital bookings. Clothes and furniture to buy in preparation for their new arrival…for Mel's expanding body.

He hated to admit it, but he was out of his depth. And just a little alarmed. He probably shouldn't have clicked to enlarge those images.

Chapped and bleeding nipples were not something he ever wanted to see again. He'd be sure they did everything to prevent Mel from suffering like that.

"Grady?"

"Yeah." He put the computer down and moved to the bed. "I'm here."

"What are you doing?" Mel reached for her water and took a sip.

"Looking online for what to do next."

"Leave it until morning." She stretched her hand out to him. "It's not like we can do anything with the information at this hour."

She was right. Besides, he had the sudden urge to hold her close. "How's the stomach?"

"It's okay. At least I'm not rushing for the bathroom."

"There's a bucket on the floor on your side," he said as he climbed under the covers.

"Oh. Thanks."

He pulled her toward him. Tucked her into his side, her head on his chest. "I want to be there for *you*. Not just the baby. I need you to know that."

"Okay."

"I'm serious. The baby ups the ante on what's between us, but I'd still want to be here, in bed with you, if you weren't pregnant." He needed her to understand this wasn't only about the baby. Needed to be sure she didn't forget it.

"I would too."

He sighed. "Get some sleep. We'll talk more in the morning."

She snuggled into him and soon dozed off. He, on the other hand, lay wondering how he was going to convince her to marry him—or at least move in with him—before she got much further alone in her pregnancy.

He planned to be there every step of the way and that would be easier if they lived in the same house.

CHAPTER 21

"I TOLD you you'd be recognized," Mel whispered.

Grady smiled. "I'm not worried."

"You should be." She glanced around the waiting room. Noticed everyone looking at them. "If someone tells the media—"

"Right now, my priority is you. I don't care what anyone else does."

She growled in frustration. "Dammit, Grady."

He leaned in, slipped his arm around her, and pulled her close. "Relax. Let's worry about one thing at a time. Right now, it's having your doctor confirm you're pregnant and finding out how to get you some relief from the morning sickness."

"You don't need to be—"

"I told you, I'm here every step of the way." He gave her a squeeze, rubbing his hand up and down her arm. "I wish I'd been there before now."

Damn. She sighed. "We didn't know."

"We do now."

"Not officially."

"We *know*."

Yeah, they did.

This morning, after she'd called her doctor's office and secured an emergency appointment, they'd scoured the Internet for information. Made a list of books they wanted to buy and started a list of baby needs that began with diapers and went to cribs and car seats.

Who knew a child could need so much? Or that there were so many choices?

"Melinda," a nurse called from the door next to the reception desk.

"That's us." Grady got to his feet, helping Mel to hers. "Can I come in, or would you prefer I wait out here?"

Jesus. This guy.

He kept tugging at her heartstrings. She knew he wanted to be there for everything but he was prepared to *not* be if it was what she wanted.

God, what *did* she want?

Only a few weeks ago she'd bemoaned the lack of princes and now she'd somehow managed to not only find one, but also tie herself to him in the most permanent of ways.

Their child would be an unbreakable connection and whether they ended up together or not, she had no right to keep Grady from that child. And that included all the months before they got to hold their baby in their arms.

Mel slipped her hand into his. "I want you with me."

He smiled. The knee-melting smiled that never failed to get her hormones jumping, except with pregnancy came an extra supply, magnifying her responses.

She couldn't decide if she wanted to pledge her undying love or push him to the floor and have her way with him right there in the waiting room.

Hands joined, they entered the exam room. The nurse put Mel's file on the desk and moved to the dreaded scales.

"Let's check a few things before Dr. Bligh comes in."

Mel went through the motions. Weight, blood pressure, temperature—the indignity of peeing in a cup.

Luckily she got to do the last one in private.

She placed the cup on the small counter in the bathroom for the nurse to collect and stepped back into the exam room.

"I'll take the sample for testing. Pop into the gown while you wait for Dr. Bligh. She won't be long." Pee cup in hand, the nurse left them alone.

"You okay?" Grady asked.

"Yeah." She took a deep breath and stripped out of her top. "Everything changes from here."

He helped her put on the gown. "It changed weeks ago."

"I suppose." Undoing her jeans, she let them drop to the floor.

"Come here." Grady held her hand while she toed off her shoes and stepped out of her pants, then he pulled her into his arms. "It's going to be fine."

Mel laughed. "Oh yeah, it'll be fine. I'm thirty years old, single, and knocked up."

"First, age is irrelevant. Second, you're not single—" He placed a finger over her lips and stopped her protest. "And third, you're going to be a terrific mother."

"Seriously. Whatever it is you're taking, I want some."

"It's called 'looking on the bright side'."

She eyed him. "I don't understand why you're not pissed off."

Grady shrugged. "Will that change anything?"

"Well, no...but still. I expected you to at least blame me or something."

"Hey, unless I'm remembering it wrong, I was *definitely*

happy to be there when we made this baby." For the first time since they'd taken the home test, Grady placed his hand on her lower stomach. "This little bit that's growing inside you is as much my doing as yours."

Her eyes filled with tears and she blinked quickly to hold them back. "God. Grady." She lowered her forehead to his chest. "Stupid pregnancy hormones. I'm not a crier."

He chuckled, the sound vibrating through his chest into her head.

"It's not funny," she grumbled.

"No. Probably not."

Mel leaned back, eyes narrowed.

He let her go and put his hands up. "Don't shoot. I held your hair out of the way, remember?"

Damn him. He had a point.

Who in their right mind would kill the guy willing to clean you up when you were sick? Even if he laughed at you when you cried?

"Fine. You get a stay of execution. For now."

Dr. Bligh chose that moment to enter the room. "Melinda, Fiona tells me there's a problem with your contraception," the woman said as she charged in, white coat flapping open.

"Yeah. It doesn't work," Mel said under her breath.

"What?" Dr. Bligh stared at her. "Doesn't work?"

"I took one of those home-test things. I'm pregnant."

"When was your last period?"

"Eight weeks ago."

"And you're sexually active." The doctor glanced at Grady and shook her head. "Forget I asked that."

A quiet tap on the door preceded the nurse. "The urine test results." She held out a sheet of paper.

Dr. Bligh scanned it and looked up. "Right. You're pregnant. First thing to do is stop taking the pill."

"I think the vomiting has taken care of that," Mel grumbled.

"Is there something she can take for the nausea?" Grady asked. Until now he'd been quietly standing behind her, hands on her shoulders. "She's lost weight because she's not keeping anything down."

"I see that." The doctor was reading over her file. "Everything else looks good though. Blood pressure isn't elevated. Hop up on the table and let me feel your abdomen. We'll work out how far along you are in a minute."

"Seven weeks."

"You sound certain." Dr. Bligh washed her hands in the small sink in the corner of the room while Grady helped Mel up onto the exam table.

"I've had sex once in the last ten months. Seven weeks ago."

"We might not hear a heartbeat yet then," the doctor said as she moved beside Mel's hip.

Mel already knew that. It was one of the things they'd discovered in their information search. They'd have to wait another few weeks because the baby's heart only started beating around the six-week mark and often wasn't heard for a few weeks after that.

Grady squeezed her hand and she glanced up to see him smiling at her.

Having him here felt good.

As much as she was capable of doing this herself, it was better having someone hold her hand.

CHAPTER 22

MEL LAY BACK while the doctor poked and prodded at her stomach. Grady stood next to her, held her hand in his and waited for the exam to be finished.

He had so many questions.

"All right. Everything feels normal." The doctor patted Mel's leg. "You can get dressed now."

Grady helped Mel up. "What do we do now, Dr. Bligh?" he asked as he handed Mel her jeans.

"You said morning sickness has been a problem?"

"Yeah, I thought I had the flu." Mel dropped the gown to the bed and pulled her top over her head. "I can't keep anything down."

"You've lost ten pounds since your last visit. I'll prescribe something but I'll also give you a list of alternative treatments. I know some mothers are very particular about what they take during their pregnancy."

"Does she need to stop doing anything?" Grady asked.

"No." The doctor held out her hand. "And maybe we should introduce ourselves?"

"Oh. Sorry." He smiled and shook the offered hand. "Grady Murdock."

"I thought you looked familiar. Storm receiver, right?"

He nodded. "Yeah. Second year."

"Brilliant touchdown last night. Saved the game with that one."

"Um...Dr. Bligh?" Mel moved beside him. "I know this goes without saying, but could we keep a lid on why I'm here today? With Grady?"

"Of course."

"Mel..."

Mel squeezed his arm. "You don't want this getting out to the media."

"I told you I'm not worried about that. You're my priority. You and the baby."

"I can't guarantee the patients in the waiting room won't somehow spread the word about you being here, but no one on my staff will reveal the nature of your visit," Dr. Bligh reassured them.

"Thanks." Mel smiled.

"Right. Let's get you what you need. Pamphlets, prenatal vitamins, blood work."

"Blood work?" Mel paled beside him.

"Yes. To confirm the pregnancy and check a number of things."

"Oh." Mel wobbled. "I think—" She raced for the bathroom.

Grady followed. Crouching next to her, he scooped her hair back and held it out of the way.

"I'll get you some water," Dr. Bligh said behind him.

The vomiting didn't last long and didn't produce more than a little bile and her breakfast. Mel hadn't eaten more than a quarter of a piece of dry toast and now that was history.

They needed to get this under control or she'd end up in the hospital.

"Perhaps we'll lay you down when we draw blood," the nurse said as she handed him a wet cloth.

Between the two of them, they got Mel out of the bathroom and on the examination table so the doctor could take the necessary samples of blood.

"Is it safe to take that much?" Grady asked as Dr. Bligh handed the nurse a third full vial.

"Yes. I'm prescribing vitamins, which will help build the baby and her blood back up." She removed the needle from Mel's arm and pressed a wad of cotton to the small puncture wound. "Hold that," she directed him.

Mel had her other arm draped over her face, her eyes closed, and she was taking slow, deep breaths. "You okay?" he asked.

"Yeah." She licked her lips. "Could use some water."

The nurse handed him a cup and relieved him of his pressure-bandage duties to apply a gauze strip to Mel's arm. "When you're ready, I'll help you sit up," she said.

Grady waited, cup of water in hand, while the doctor labeled vials and the nurse helped Mel sit up.

"All right. We're good. I'll get Fiona to get that literature for you and make an appointment for Thursday morning. If you haven't kept anything down by then, I'll reassess and possibly give you some fluids intravenously. Between now and Thursday, you're on bed rest. Or in this case, park your butt and don't go running any marathons—and that includes managing any events."

Grady grinned as Mel scowled.

"I have a business to run," she argued.

"Yes, and I happen to know, as I've used your services a

time or two, that you have very competent staff to hold down the fort while you take it easy and build some strength back up." Dr. Bligh held out her hand to Grady. "It was great to meet you and I'm sure I'll be seeing you again. And congratulations to you both."

Grady smiled. "Thanks."

"See you both Thursday."

After the doctor left and the nurse gave them a bag full of things to read and their appointment time for Thursday, Grady took Mel home.

He set her up on the couch, remote in hand, glass of water close, and proceeded to pamper her to the point she yelled at him to leave her alone.

He only smiled.

It didn't matter how much she shouted at him, the thought of her growing their baby inside her had him grinning like a fool.

CHAPTER 23

SIX DAYS LATER...

MEL TOOK her first easy breath in nearly a week. "So I can go back to normal hours?"

"A normal person's normal hours, yes. Don't overdo it. You've only put on two of the pounds you lost and you're building a baby as well as regaining your strength. Don't rush back in."

"I'll make sure she takes care of herself," Grady said.

Dr. Bligh smiled. "I'm sure you will. I want to see you again in a few weeks to see if we can't get a listen to that heartbeat. I know you were hoping for that today."

"I was but you said everything is fine so I can wait a while longer," Mel said. Grady squeezed her hand and she smiled at him, grateful for his reassuring presence.

"Your blood work came back normal. You're keeping food down and the nausea isn't as severe. I think you're well on the way to good health." Dr. Bligh passed her a business card. "Here's the OBGYN I was telling you about. Dr. Nevins. Give her office a call and make an appointment."

"Thanks." Grady stood. "We'll see you in three weeks."

"Yes. Thank you." Mel got to her feet.

"You're welcome."

They left Dr. Bligh's office and, like the two other times they'd been there, quickly made their way to Grady's SUV.

"We should have brought my car. It's less conspicuous," Mel said as she climbed in.

"I need to drop you off at the office and head straight to the arena." Grady got them on the road without much difficulty. Despite driving a huge tank of a vehicle, he maneuvered it as though it were Matchbox-car sized. "I'm going to be late for training as it is."

"You shouldn't have come then." She hated that he was putting himself out for her.

"Don't be silly. You know I want to be there whenever I can. It's bad enough I have to go out of town some weeks."

"I'll be fine."

"I know you will. I just want to be with you."

He'd been so attentive since they'd found out she was pregnant. Made sure she ate well, brought her vitamins and spent every second he could with her.

Luckily his schedule had allowed it. He'd had a game at home last night but later this week he was out of town for a Sunday night game.

"I'll pick you up after training. That should give you plenty of time to immerse yourself back into work." He shot a grin her way. "Not that you haven't been working from your couch."

She smiled. She'd convinced him going home to rest was the best thing for her. All her stuff was there. And Carla had been happy to drop in most afternoons and run through what was happening at work.

It meant she hadn't felt out of the loop. Or bored out of

her mind. "I didn't work that much." Carla and Davie hadn't let her.

"Not for lack of trying." Grady turned into the parking lot in front of her office. "I'll be about four hours."

"Okay." Mel opened her door when the car stopped.

"Wait. I'll walk you in."

"Grady, I'm fine."

He sighed. "You're a pain in the ass, you know."

"Why? Because I don't want to be treated like spun glass? Like I'll fall apart if you're not with me?"

Frowning, he said, "I'll watch you go in."

Figuring she wasn't going to win this battle, she leaned over and dropped a quick kiss on his mouth. "Thanks for caring."

His hand wrapped around the back of her neck and held her close. "Don't forget that I do."

That wasn't likely. He did things for her without asking, it seemed as though without thought.

Little things like refilling her glass of water when he noticed it was low. Big things like holding her hand while she waited to hear what the doctor had to say.

He'd been with her almost twenty-four-seven for the last six days—hell, he'd just about moved in with her—and she'd been surprisingly comfortable with it.

Smiling, she pulled away. "I won't."

Climbing out of the car, she closed the door and walked across the parking lot. Waving, she headed inside—and was instantly surrounded.

"Should you be at work?"

"How are you feeling?"

"You look better than last time I saw you."

The last was from Davie. He hadn't seen her since dropping her at home.

She smiled at him. "I'm much better."

He leaned in close so only she could hear. "We kept it quiet. The staff thinks you had a really bad intestinal bug."

Mel wasn't sure if the news of her pregnancy getting out was worse than the staff thinking *that* or not. "Thanks."

"Come and sit down." Carla grabbed her elbow and steered her toward her office. "I'm sure you all have work to do," she called over her shoulder as she marched them through the gathered staff.

With a sigh, Mel sank into her chair. Carla had shut the door when they'd come in so they had some privacy. "I'm sorry to put you through all this drama."

"Nonsense." Carla dropped into the seat opposite Mel's desk. "It's my job."

"It's not your job to carry the business." Mel was grateful, more than, but ultimately Carla was just an employee.

"I'm not carrying it."

Mel held up a hand. "Let me finish. I appreciate everything you do, have done, in the years since I first started out but this last week has made me realize how much I've held tight to control and not given you the rewards or accolades you're due."

"You've given me plenty of bonuses and you pay me way above industry standard."

"I do. But that's for selfish reasons. I didn't want anyone to poach you." She smiled. "And to make sure no one ever does, I've got a proposition for you."

Carla arched one blonde eyebrow. "What kind of proposition?"

"I want you to consider taking part ownership of the company."

"What?" Carla was on her feet. "Are you mad?"

"No. I think it's one of the soundest business decisions

I've made. We'll ignore the fact I should have done this sooner."

"But—"

"Let's be honest. I'm going to have a lot of my time taken up by a small human in about seven months' time and I can't be as hands-on as I have been in the past. Who knows?" She shrugged. "I might want to work part-time or not at all once the baby comes."

"I still don't think—"

Her office door burst open and Davie barreled in. "We've got a problem, boss." He darted a look over his shoulder.

"Think about it, Carla." Standing, Mel walked around her desk. "What could you possibly not handle, Davie?"

"An office full of paparazzi."

CHAPTER 24

Grady had just removed his shirt and was reaching for his practice jersey when Coach Bane yelled at him.

"Murdock. Front office wants to see you."

"Uh-oh, Grade A, what have you done now?" Sawyer asked.

He pulled his shirt back on and shrugged. "No idea."

"Now, Murdock. Best not to keep the big boss waiting."

Mark Mitchum wanted to see him?

"Can't be good if he's pulling you from training," Garrett said beside him.

"Guess I should go find out."

It was probably some media thing they wanted him involved with. Ever since that last-minute touchdown, the press had been touting him as the man with all the moves on the field.

Coach Bane fell into step beside him but it wasn't until they both got into the elevator that Grady realized he was being escorted upstairs.

What the fuck had he done?

"So what's this about?" he asked.

"Best to wait for the boss."

As usual, Coach was a man of few words when it didn't pertain to football plays.

They entered the reception area of the front office and were instantly ushered through to a large conference room.

Mark Mitchum, Connor Wade, Lexi Mitchum, and TJ Boldt all sat around the big table.

The club's president and vice president, VP of public relations, and VP of player personnel in one room did not bode well for him.

"Take a seat, Mr. Murdock." Mark Mitchum gestured to the seat opposite him.

Grady swallowed hard and sat. No one offered him their usual smile. He glanced at all the serious faces and figured whatever had brought them all here couldn't be good.

"Do you have something you want to tell us?" Mark asked.

"Ah, no." He held the other man's gaze. "Should I? If you could give me a hint..."

Mark nodded at Lexi, who pushed an iPad across the table toward him.

Looking down, Grady found a grainy, blurred photo of himself and Mel leaving the doctor's office this morning.

"How'd you get this?" he asked, his eyes glued to the picture.

"It's splashed all over the Internet." Lexi leaned over and tapped the screen. "Along with this interesting headline."

THE MAN WITH ALL THE MOVES ON THE FIELD
PROVES HE HAS THEM OFF. GRADY MURDOCK,
MIAMI STORM'S GOLDEN BOY, HAS GOTTEN A
LITTLE TARNISHED.

He scrolled down to read the article. He didn't get further than the first sentence—and Mel's name—before he was on his feet.

"Shit! I have to go."

"Whoa." Conner rose and moved toward him. "Slow down."

"I have to get to Mel. If they've got her name, they know where she works. She doesn't need the media in her face right now."

"Murdock, I think you should be more worried about yourself," Mark said behind him.

"I'm not the one who's just come off bed rest." He made for the door.

"You walk out that door, Murdock, and you can kiss your multi-million-dollar contract goodbye."

Grady stopped and turned at Mark's words. "You're kidding?"

"No." Mark stood and crossed his arms. "I never joke about contracts. Sit down and explain why the fuck I'm finding out from the fucking media that one of my star receivers has knocked up some woman."

"She's not *some woman*."

"I know who the hell she is, Murdock. I hired her, remember?" Mark's voice rose a few levels with every word.

Sighing, Grady ran a hand down his face. "I swear, I'll explain everything, but I need to get to Mel before the media does."

"Too late."

"What?"

"She called me the minute they showed up at her office. They must have missed you by seconds. And since then there is a horde of them outside the arena."

"I have to—"

"No, you don't." Mark let out a breath and dropped into his chair. "My security team is organizing her transportation here."

"They should be here in the next ten minutes," Lexi added. "Luckily, Steve Goodman was close by her office and he's dealing with the media and bringing her to the arena."

"Oh." Relief dropped his shoulders. "She's okay?"

"As far as I know," Mark said, indicating the chair opposite him again. "Sit down, Grady. You can take the time until they get here to explain what the hell is going on between my star receiver and my event planner."

Grady figured that wouldn't be the only demand for an explanation he'd get today if Mel's pregnancy was splashed all over the news.

And funnily enough, Mark Mitchum didn't scare him anywhere near as much as his mother did.

CHAPTER 25

FOUR DAYS LATER...

"Do we really have to do this now?" she asked as Grady drove them to the airport to pick up his parents.

"If we don't, she'll just hunt us down. It's best to get it over with in a public place."

Oh, that thought made Mel feel a whole lot better. Her queasy stomach rolled. "They're going to hate me."

"Bullshit." He turned into the parking lot. "You're carrying their first grandchild. They'll worship the ground you walk on. Trust me."

"I doubt that," she murmured.

It had been four days since the media went crazy—and things hadn't calmed down yet. In that time, she'd been forced to move in with Grady and work from home.

The paparazzi were worse than vultures. They hid behind bushes. Searched in her garbage and shoved their cameras and microphones in her face.

And she didn't even want to think about the long-range lenses that seemed to be trained on her all day, if the number of grainy photos hitting the Internet were to be explained.

"Hey." Grady found a spot and parked. Turning to face her, he grabbed her hand with both of his. "It's going to be okay. I promise."

"Yeah. I'm sure an unplanned pregnancy with a woman you barely know is exactly what your parents wished for you."

"Stop." He squeezed her hand. "I'll keep saying it until you believe me, Mel. I'd be here without Little Bit growing in your belly."

"I don't think we'd be at the meet-the-parents stage yet."

"No. Probably not. But we are, so we deal with it."

"How can you be so calm about this?" She yanked her hand from his and got out of the car. He met her at her door before she got the damn thing closed.

"Hey, hey. Come here." He pulled her into his arms, his big hands smoothing up and down her back and her muscles instantly softened. Why did this man's embrace soothe her so easily? "Everything will work out."

"God. You're always so optimistic."

"And you're always so pessimistic." He kissed the top of her head. "We're the perfect balance."

Were they? She didn't have a clue. And the stupid pregnancy hormones weren't helping her make rational decisions. She couldn't be sure of her true feelings when her emotions had been hijacked by *Little Bit*, as Grady kept referring to the baby.

"Grady."

"One day at a time, Mel. You promised me."

She had. She'd given her word, and regardless of the fear slicing through her every other minute or the second-guessing, she'd honor that vow.

It wasn't the one he wanted from her, they both knew that, but for now it would have to be enough. Taking a deep breath, she eased out of his arms.

"I did promise. And I'll try to remember that when the dark clouds creep over." She forced a smile and wove her fingers through his. "Let's go face the evil genius who made you put itching powder in your own underwear."

Grady groaned. "Did you have to bring that up?"

Mel laughed. It felt good to enjoy the moment for a change. She'd been so bogged down in sickness and shock and adjustment that she'd forgotten to enjoy herself.

She was turning into someone she didn't recognize. With her indecision and reliance on others, she was becoming someone she didn't like.

Time to find the woman she'd been before her world got turned upside down and inside out.

Grady tugged on her hand. "It's good to hear that sound. Haven't in a few weeks."

She smiled. "I know. Sorry."

"No need to apologize. You've had a lot going on." He let go of her hand to wrap his arm around her shoulders and tuck her against his side. "We'll just have to find things to make you laugh more often from now on."

They entered the terminal and Grady used his big body to shield her from the rushing crowd. "I forgot how busy it is on a Friday night," she said as she burrowed in closer to him.

"Maybe you should have stayed home." He shoved a hand out to stop a businessman from crashing into her. "Hey. Watch it."

"Sorry," the man said before continuing on his journey.

Mel shook her head. "I'm going to pretend he's been away for work the last month and he's in a hurry to get home to his wife and five kids."

Grady laughed. "Or he's an ass and on his way to a local bar for a pick up."

"Wow. Did we just swap roles? I'm now the optimist and

you're the pessimist?"

"See? Perfectly balanced." He grinned down at her. "This way. Their plane should have landed."

"Are we late?"

"No. I didn't want to hang around too long. We don't need any more attention than we've already had this week."

"True." Mel ducked her head and let Grady guide them to the gate his parents would be disembarking through. "Although you're a little hard to miss...not sure you'd be inconspicuous no matter how long you spent in one place."

"Well, we've got backup if there's a problem."

Her head snapped up and she stared at Grady. "Backup?"

"Yeah. Mark Mitchum insisted. There's a couple of his security guys around here somewhere."

She jerked her head around, her gaze swinging over the crowd quickly. "Where?"

Grady shrugged. "No idea. They followed us in and are only supposed to make their presence known if we hit any trouble with the media."

"Do you think we will?" Mel turned back to Grady.

"It's possible. But let's not worry about that. There's Mom and Dad."

Mel looked up and saw into the future.

Coming toward them was a man the very image of Grady, only about twenty years older. The woman beside him was tiny. There was no way she was more than five feet tall.

"Grady!"

Mel stepped aside as his mother launched herself at him. With a skill that spoke of years of practice, he caught her mid-leap and held her off the ground.

Watching the genuine love between them brought tears to Mel's eyes. "Stupid pregnancy hormones."

"Now, there isn't anything stupid about making a baby."

Grady's dad smiled down at her.

She smiled sheepishly in return. "Sorry. Didn't mean to say that out loud."

"You must be Mel." He glanced at his wife and son. "Put her down now, Grady, and introduce us to this lovely woman —who, I might add, looks much better in real life than those crappy pictures in the tabloids."

"Oh, yes. Put me down. I want to get a look at the mother of my grandchild."

Mel's face flushed. "Hi." She gave a little finger wave and instantly felt like an idiot.

Grady pulled her close and slid an arm around her. "Mom, Dad, this is Melinda Shaw. Mel, my mom and dad, Sarah and Archie."

"Your father is right. She's far prettier than those horrible photos showed." Grady's mom smiled at her while opening her arms. "Let me give you a hug. I'm so excited to spend the next few weeks getting to know you."

"A few weeks?" Mel looked up at Grady as she was enveloped in a sweet-smelling embrace.

"Yeah, they're staying until after my next three away games."

"I told you I'd be fine."

"I know."

"But—"

"Let's get going. I think we've been spotted," Grady's father said.

Mel looked around to see a man aiming a camera with a long lens in their direction. She frowned. "Someone else needs to do something scandalous so they leave us alone."

Grady laughed. "I'll see if I can convince Garrett or Sawyer or maybe one of the new rookies, to do something over the weekend."

CHAPTER 26

GRADY LEANED against the wall and listened to his parents talking with Mel. She was laughing. Having a good time. She'd even managed to finish a whole plate of his mother's chicken pie.

A big improvement on her eating of late. She was slowly regaining the weight she'd lost and the sparkle in her eyes was showing up more and more too.

He'd missed this Mel. The funny, independent, take-control, confident woman he'd discovered during the weeks following their first night together hadn't been seen since she'd become sick.

She'd been so drained by the pregnancy so far. He still wished he could have made that easier for her.

She was improving with every day. Finally he was seeing what people referred to as the *glow of pregnancy*.

Her laughter rang out and Grady smiled.

"What are you doing hiding out in here?" his dad asked as he entered the kitchen.

Grady straightened off the wall. "Giving you guys a few minutes alone."

"You think we need that?"

"Yes." He shook his head. "No. Maybe."

"I like her." His dad glanced over his shoulder. "And I'm pretty sure your mother is in love and liable to throw you over for Mel as the favorite."

Grady chuckled. "I'm pretty sure you're Mom's favorite."

His dad held up his hands. "Nope. I'm not the one carrying her grandchild."

"I know this isn't happening the way you expected—"

"Not another word, Grady. All your mother and I ever want is for you kids to be happy. This woman, Mel, she makes you happy. We both see that."

"You do?"

His father smiled. "Yeah. It's the way you are with her. The way you look at her like she holds the sun and moon in her hands. Whether you've worked it out or not yet, you're in love with her. And I don't think it's because you put a baby in her belly."

"No." He thought back over the weeks since he and Mel had met. "I think I fell the first night we spent together. But that's too fast, right?"

"For some people, yes. For you? No. You've always been quick to set your mind to something and go after it with your whole heart."

"I don't want to screw this up. She won't marry me or move in..."

"Seems to me you've accomplished the second one already."

"That's only to keep her safe from the media. They've been crazy since the story broke."

"You did the right thing there, Mel and the baby need to be under as little stress as possible until she gets over the morning sickness. Now you need to make the most of her being here. Show her staying with you is the best thing for her and the baby."

"Easier said than done, Dad."

"Don't I know it? Your Mel reminds me of your mother. Independent and used to making her own decisions. Which is why you need to get her thinking it's *her* idea to stay."

"I don't think that'll work. She already thinks she's forcing me into being with her because of Little Bit."

"So you treat her as though she isn't carrying your baby."

"Hard when my baby makes her throw up her breakfast just about every day."

"Never said it would be easy, Grady. You know nothing worth having comes without work."

"And yet it was no work at all to fall for Mel." Grady grinned. "I swear, I barely clapped eyes on her and I was a goner."

"There's no denying she's special, son."

"I don't know what I'll do if I lose her, Dad."

The thought of Mel not being in his life, of only having contact with her because of their child, made his blood run cold, tightened every muscle, and twisted his gut to the point of pain.

"Then let's make sure she knows what she's giving up if she walks away."

He knew his dad meant well but it wasn't up to his parents to convince Mel to stay.

No.

That was all on him.

CHAPTER 27

SIXTEEN DAYS LATER...

MEL PROWLED through Grady's house. His parents were in bed but she couldn't sleep. She was restless. Grady was away.

Again.

The Storm were playing the New York Dragons and weren't due back until tomorrow.

He'd only been gone one night this trip and no matter how many times she walked into his bedroom, she couldn't make herself climb into bed without him.

The couch wasn't nearly as comfortable as his bed but it's where she'd been sleeping the nights he was away.

She'd grown used to him being beside her. Unless he had training or a game, he'd been with her twenty-four-seven for a couple of weeks now, ever since the media had splashed their names all over, and she'd become so accustomed to him being around that she didn't know what to do with herself when he wasn't.

Work had kept her busy, not that she'd been in the office much, she'd been doing most of her work remotely, and today she'd had lunch out at her favorite Greek restaurant with Grady's parents.

Sarah and Archie Murdock managed to distract her with tales of Grady's youth, but now that she was alone again...

She missed him.

Watching the replay of the game was out. Last time she'd seen Grady play, he'd taken a hard hit and she'd barely kept her dinner down.

She'd rather not experience that again.

"Having trouble sleeping?" Grady's mother entered the kitchen behind her.

Mel stared at her. "I can't stay."

She slapped a hand over her mouth. Where those words came from, she didn't know.

"Oh?" Sarah moved to the stove and checked the water level in the kettle. "I think this calls for tea."

"Sarah—"

"Tea first."

They were quiet while they worked together making the tea. Mel's mind whirled with thoughts and the only one she could catch hold of was that she'd trapped Grady.

He didn't need her—not like she was beginning to need him.

Sitting at the counter, Mel took a sip of the hot, sweet tea Sarah put in front of her.

"Why can't you stay?" Sarah asked as she sat next to Mel, her own cup in hand.

"I've forced him into this."

"No. You've *both* been forced into it."

"He's got the rest of his life—"

"So have you."

"I'm thirty."

"Oh my gosh, you're positively ancient." Sarah placed a hand on her chest. "We should order your walker right now."

"I'm serious," Mel argued. Normally she'd find Sarah's sense of humor funny. Not tonight.

"No. You're making excuses. Whatever you can think of. What is it you're really afraid of, Mel? That Grady is with you only because you're pregnant—or that you're in love with him?"

"I...that's not...I don't..." Mel stopped. Sarah wasn't only an evil genius. She was psychic.

"Loving someone doesn't weaken you, Mel. It makes you stronger. You're missing him because you want him around, not because you can't survive without him."

"Then why does it feel like there's a steel band around my chest? Like I can't catch my breath?"

"Because you've been thrown into this without warning. You've been sick, you've got a crazy bunch of hormones hijacking your system, the media chasing you, and while you're dealing with all that, you're trying to adjust to a life that includes someone else. None of those are easy things to do on their own; throw them all together at once and you're in for a bit of work."

"I don't know if I can do this." The idea of failing...of disappointing Grady.

"Nobody does. There are no guarantees in life. But if we *never* try, we always fail." Sarah placed her hand over Mel's. "I can't tell you if the two of you will make it or not, but I *can* tell you that my son loves you. And while Little Bit might have something to do with that, it isn't what started those feelings."

"How can I be sure?"

"You can't. You have to have faith. In him. In you."

She wanted to. Wanted to believe they could build a life together. "I don't want to hurt him."

"The only way you'll do that is if you give up without trying. Grady's always been very determined, worked his ass off for whatever he wanted. He'd expect no less from the woman in his life."

"That's just it. I don't know if that's me."

Sarah patted her hand. "I have enough faith for both of you."

"I wish that was all we needed."

"Why don't you take that tea to bed? Read a book or watch some TV. Find something that will relax you and stop that brain of yours from spinning for a while." Sarah got to her feet. "Grady will be home tomorrow and you can talk to him about your concerns. I always find voicing my worries to Archie helps me work through them. Sometimes he has answers and sometimes just having him listen to me is enough to solve the problem."

"I do have some episodes of *Supernatural* I haven't watched."

That was a lie.

In the last few weeks she'd watched all of them during Grady's away games; it was how she'd been spending her nights without him and explaining why she was on the couch each morning when Archie found her.

"Good girl." Sarah helped Mel to her feet, linking their arms. "Let's walk together."

"Are you mothering me, Sarah?"

"Is it an issue if I am?"

Mel smiled at Grady's mom. "No. It's actually nice."

"Well, then. Expect to be mothered from now on."

"I'd like that." There hadn't been a lot of affection in her life.

Mel didn't remember much about her mother, whether she was a hugger or not, and her grandmother had been a quiet, timid woman who kowtowed to her grandfather. No hugs or coddling from her because it made for a weak spine according to him.

But she'd learned over the last couple weeks that the Murdocks were very affectionate, and not opposed to public displays of it.

In fact, since meeting Grady, she'd received more cuddles, touches, hand holding, and random kisses than in the previous thirty years of her life.

CHAPTER 28

GRADY LET himself into the house through the front door. He knew Mel was at the office—he'd spoken to her as soon as the plane landed—but his parents should be home. "Mom? Dad?"

"In the kitchen," his mom yelled.

He grinned. It had been years since he'd come home to that. "Are there cookies?" he yelled back.

"And milk!" came her answer.

He laughed. "I'd rather a beer."

"Not before midday." His mother strode into the hall. "Is that full of laundry?"

"Yeah, I'll throw it on in a minute."

"Give it to me. I'll deal with it before Mel comes home and finds out you're a slob."

"That's a lie and you know it. Anyway, Mel's worse than me."

Mel was the slob. Well, not really, but out of the two of them, Grady was definitely the neat freak. Funny considering her work life required complete organization, right down to where the last paper clip was.

"She is somewhat domestically disordered." Mom smiled. "But God, she can cook."

"She can?" In all the time they'd spent together, he'd cooked or they'd ordered out.

"She's never cooked for you?"

He shook his head.

"Well, she opened cupboards, the fridge and freezer, and pulled together a chicken penne dish more delicious than any I've eaten in an Italian restaurant. There are some leftovers if you want me to heat them up for you."

"Snack size or meal size?"

She grinned at him. "Snack. You can have some of the cookies I baked for dessert."

Grady groaned. "If you keep making cookies I'll turn into a lard-ass and lose my job."

"Never. I've seen you train. You're in no danger from my cookies."

"Probably not." He pressed a kiss to his mom's head. "I'll grab a quick shower then throw a load in the washer. Meet you in the kitchen."

"Okay. Your father should be back soon."

"Where is he?"

"Picking up a few things."

"Oh?"

"Nothing you need to worry about right now."

Grady eyed his mother. She was up to something. "Am I going to be mad?"

She shrugged. "Possibly."

"Mom."

She held up a hand. "It's a grandparent's prerogative."

"Oh God." He turned toward his room. "I don't want to know."

Her laughter followed him into his bathroom. He hoped whatever his parents had done didn't upset Mel.

She'd seemed a little shaky on the phone earlier. He'd thought they'd found their footing recently but something had happened while he was away this time.

Something had spooked her. He'd learned to read her pretty well over the course of the last few weeks. She was stressed and it wasn't the baby this time.

It was him.

Showered and changed, he headed for the kitchen. Voices filled the house, his mother's, one that seemed familiar, and one he didn't recognize...

"Grady." His mother gestured for him to come in, which was weird, considering this was his house. "Come say hello to Alex and Sadie."

"Alex?" Grady stepped into the kitchen and made a beeline for his cousin. "Hey, man, what are you doing in Miami?"

"Had a meeting earlier." They did the hug, back slap thing. "I see your moves are making headlines."

Grady grimaced. "Yeah, on and off the field." He turned to Alex's wife. "Lovely to see you again." He'd only met his cousin's wife once before. At their wedding. Three years ago. Jeez, he really needed to make the effort to go home more often.

"Lovely to see you again too. I'm looking forward to seeing more of you now that you're with Mel."

"With Mel? Wait. Sadie?" His brain clicked through information. He couldn't believe he hadn't joined the dots before now. "Mel's *friend* Sadie? The one that lives in New York?

Except she meant the state and I thought she meant the city..."

Sadie grinned at him. "I didn't think either of you had worked out the connection yet. If you had, Mel would have said something. When Alex said he had a meeting down here, I couldn't pass up the chance to visit."

Fuck.

Mel was the maid of honor. The one he'd drooled over at Alex's wedding. Not that he'd said anything about it to anyone.

He'd been twenty-one the first time he'd set eyes on Mel and he'd known.

Dammit, he'd *known*.

"So how long are you in town?" he asked.

"It was supposed to be a day but Sadie convinced me to stay overnight so she can spend some 'girl time' with Mel." Alex glanced at his wife, who smiled and slid her arm around his waist.

Grady felt a little sting of envy at their obvious closeness. "Does Mel know you're coming?"

"No. It was last minute and I wanted to surprise her," Sadie said.

Grady laughed. "In my experience, she doesn't do so well with surprises."

"She used to love them." Sadie grinned. "Besides, she'll be too excited to see me to be annoyed."

"I hope so." Grady looked at his mom. "Dad back yet?"

"No. When Sadie and Alex arrived, I called him and told him to pick Mel up early."

"And she agreed to that?" He knew she hated being pulled away from work early. The woman was a workaholic.

"Oh, I didn't ask and your father is going to pretend he got the time wrong and guilt her into leaving." She smiled and

Grady was reminded of her master's level skills of manipulation.

"Dear God. She doesn't stand a chance."

His mother patted his cheek. "No, dear. She doesn't. After dealing with you, Mel is child's play."

Deciding he was safest out of his mother's line of fire, he moved to the fridge. "Can I get anyone a drink?"

"I'd love something cold," Alex answered.

"Do you have peppermint tea? I find it settles the nausea really well," Sadie said.

Grady bolted upright. "Nausea?" he asked, staring at Sadie.

"Yes. Morning sickness." She smiled.

"Um..." Grady glanced at his mother. "When did you last speak to Mel?"

"Don't look so worried. I know you knocked her up." Sadie grinned and Alex laughed. "The whole country knows you knocked her up."

Grady lowered his head and stared at the floor, blew out a breath. "Jesus."

"Well, it's the truth," his mother added.

"Yes, but do we need to be so crude about it?" He grabbed two bottles of water.

Sadie laughed. "I love that the big bad football player can blush."

He shook his head and tossed a bottle to Alex. "They're going to be hell together, aren't they?"

Alex nodded. "Best to stay out of their way when they're together. Although this time there won't be any alcohol involved."

"Hey!" Sadie slapped at Alex's arm.

The door to the garage opened and they all looked over.

Mel stepped in, her head turned back toward his father,

who followed right behind. "I distinctly remember double checking what time you were going to pick me up."

"Memory loss. Old age." He winked at Grady over Mel's head.

"Well—" She faced forward, her steps faltering as she caught sight of them all in the kitchen. "Sadie?"

"Surprise!" Sadie flung her arms wide and Mel burst into tears.

"Shit!" Grady demolished the space between them in a millisecond. Wrapping her in his arms, he murmured in her ear, "Sh. It's okay. Don't cry."

"My God. Mel *never* cries," Sadie said, clearly astonished by her friend's emotional outburst.

"Pregnancy does crazy things to a woman," Alex muttered.

CHAPTER 29

"I still can't believe I cried when I saw you." Mel buried her face in her hands.

Sadie laughed. "What? You think I haven't cried at a leaf falling from a tree since I got pregnant? Alex is right. Pregnancy does crazy things to a woman."

"Shush." Mel glanced toward the door before moving her gaze to her best friend. "Must you say that so loud? We wouldn't want him to hear you. His head's big enough."

"I know, but I've put him through the wringer since we started trying for a baby. Months and months of fertility treatments and the ensuing roller coaster of hormonal moods, only to give up and *then* fall pregnant without any assistance. Now the baby hormones have kicked in and I'll be damned if they're not worse than the artificial lot I was pumping myself full of."

"I've missed this," Mel said.

Sadie grinned. "Me too."

"Why can't you live closer?"

"Because my husband and my job are in New York. And why couldn't you get knocked up by a New York Dragon?"

"Do you know any as hot as Grady?"

"About that…" Sadie waved a hand in front of her face. "That man is seriously smokin'. And if you tell my husband I said that, I'll deny it 'til my dying breath. I can't believe you're with Alex's cousin! Or that you never spoke at the wedding. How did that happen? You were both there, both involved. How is it you didn't hook up there but you hooked up here? Not that I'm complaining. We'll be related when you get married!" Sadie all but squealed the last part.

Mel ignored all of her best friend's questions and asked one of her own. "How did you know?"

"Know what?"

"That Alex was the one."

"Oh. Well. He didn't go away."

"That makes no sense." Mel was there for Sadie and Alex's courtship, such as it was.

They'd had a one-night stand that turned into two nights that turned into living together, followed by marriage and now a baby.

Sadie shrugged. "No matter how much I pushed him away or resisted his advances, he didn't stop. He was one determined man."

"So he wore you down?"

"No. It felt like I couldn't breathe when he wasn't around. It was as though my rib cage contracted whenever we were apart or I thought about breaking it off."

"Oh."

"Are you trying to work out if you're in love with Grady?" Sadie asked.

Mel shook her head. "No."

"Good, you've worked out you are then."

"You think I am?"

"How long have we known each other? I've never seen you look at a guy the way you look at Grady."

"How do I look at him?" She really needed to know what Sadie saw. As much as she trusted Grady's mom, she trusted Sadie more.

"Like the sun rises and sets on his shoulders. Like you want to climb his body and kiss him senseless. Like you want to stand close to him and rub your face against him. Like you—"

"Enough." Mel held up a hand. "I get it."

"Do you?"

"Yes." She could be honest with Sadie; more than with Sarah. "But I'm scared to death. I don't know what I'm doing, or what he wants or expects, and then there's the baby."

"I'll admit it's not the best of circumstances but I've seen the way he looks at you, the way he is with you. He's not doing it just because he knocked you up."

"Stop saying that!"

Sadie laughed. "Not on your life. I love that you did the one thing you continuously lectured me about in college."

"It wasn't as though we didn't try to prevent it from happening. We used two forms of contraception."

"Really? Jesus. There's me using nothing and getting nowhere all those years, and you..."

"He's obviously got super-sperm or something."

"Or you two are meant to be together and this is fate's way of guaranteeing it."

Mel stared at Sadie's smug smile. "Fate? You're a believer in fate now?"

"Kinda. I guess I just believe that there's something bigger than us steering things. Take me and Alex. There's no way we'd have ended up together if I hadn't mistaken him for Alec Dane."

"True."

"See? Some things are meant to be."

"And you think I was meant to get knocked up by Grady?" Mel asked with a smile.

"Well the knocked-up part could have waited a while, until you two were more comfortable with the way you feel about each other, but if it gets you to where you're supposed to be, I'm all for it." She grinned. "And now we get to have babies at the same time. Our kids get to grow up together."

"Except you live in a different state."

"It's the same time zone."

"But still miles away."

"Maybe not for long..."

Mel sat up. "What?"

"Alex is in Miami about a possible project that will take years to complete. If it gets the go-ahead, then we'll be moving down here for a while."

"Oh my God, are you serious?"

"They're waiting on investors. Two are already on board; they just need a third to put up some cash."

"I've got cash."

Sadie laughed. "Not this much cash."

"How much are we talking about?"

"Millions."

"Oh."

"Yeah. Oh." Sadie yawned. "Lord, I'm ready for bed and it's not even eight."

"I can't believe how much pregnancy wipes you out. I don't think I've ever slept as much as in recent weeks." Mel pushed to her feet. "We should find the men and call it a night. We've got all day tomorrow before you have to fly home."

"I'm so glad I talked Alex into taking the extra day."

"Me too." Mel offered a hand to Sadie. "C'mon, let's go find our men."

Sadie didn't say anything about Mel referring to Grady as hers but she did arch an eyebrow, so she knew her friend had noticed the unconscious slip.

Except calling him hers didn't feel like a mistake.

He felt like hers.

She just needed to learn to trust that feeling.

CHAPTER 30

FIVE DAYS LATER…

"It was lovely to meet you both." Mel hugged his mom and dad and smiled.

"The pleasure was ours," his dad said as he gave Mel an extra squeeze.

While Grady hadn't spent as much time with his parents as he would have liked, the visit had been a good one.

Three of the most important people in his life had bonded and he had to hope it was another tether between him and Mel that she wouldn't want to cut.

"We'll be back before the baby." His mom reached up and placed her hands on his cheeks. "Bend down here, you."

He smiled and did as ordered, placing his forehead against hers. It was something they'd done when he was little that she refused to give up even though he'd outgrown her by the age of twelve.

"You take care of my girls," she said.

Grady laughed. "You don't know that."

"Wishful thinking." She broke contact and went to her tiptoes to kiss his brow. "Love you, Grady."

"Love you too, Mom. Call when you get home."

"Will do." His father pulled him into a backslapping hug.

"Right. Let's go, Archie." His mother picked up her carry-on bag. "Before I embarrass myself by crying. You know I hate goodbyes."

Slipping his hand into Mel's, they stood beside the car and watched them go until they disappeared from sight.

"Alone at last," he breathed.

Mel tilted her head and cocked one eyebrow.

"What? Do you know how hard it's been keeping my hands off you?"

"We sleep in the same bed."

"Yes but my parents were sleeping down the hall!"

He helped Mel into the car and jogged around to the driver's side. As usual, traffic around the airport was mayhem and he concentrated on getting them out of there without having an accident.

Mel was suspiciously quiet beside him. He spared a glance at her before returning his gaze to the road. "You okay?"

"Have you really not touched me because your parents were in the house?"

"Ah, *yeah*." He chanced another look at her and almost rear-ended a Mini Cooper when it zipped into the lane ahead of them. He slammed on the brakes, stuck his arm out across Mel's chest in a useless attempt to keep her from flying forward. The seatbelt did its job though. "Shit. Sorry."

"So it's not because you no longer want me that way?"

Was she crying? Grady couldn't risk another look so kept his eyes straight ahead. "I'm not sure this is the best place to have this discussion, but yes, I've not laid a hand on you because my parents were here."

She sniffled.

"Jesus. Mel. Don't cry."

"I'm not," she sniffled again.

"Okay. You're not." Traffic cleared when they reached the highway. "Can we talk about this when we get home?"

"I think we should talk about other things too."

Grady didn't like the sound of that. They'd avoided all talk of them in recent weeks, just going through the motions of their lives, their jobs, dealing with the drama of the media.

His parents being around had also helped to distract both of them from facing the big question...

Where did they go from here?

He wanted to get married.

She didn't.

He wanted her to move in.

She didn't want to do that either.

Although she was pretty much living with him now.

The drive home was twenty minutes of silence. He was starting to worry Mel wanted to end things. Not that she could—or would—end the pregnancy, but still...by the time Grady pulled into the garage, he was sweating.

He switched the car off. "Mel—"

"Can we go inside?" She hopped out of the car without waiting for a reply.

Grady watched her go through the connecting door and blew out a breath. "Jesus." He scrubbed a hand down his face. No point putting it off.

Following her inside, he was surprised when he didn't find her in the kitchen. "Mel?"

"In here."

God. She was in the bedroom. Probably packing. With feet that felt as though they were made of lead, he walked to his room.

The last thing he expected to see was Mel, lying on the bed. Naked.

At the sight of her, he forgot all about talking. His body instantly hardened.

The arousal he'd been ruthlessly shoving aside the last few weeks exploded through his veins like soda from a shaken bottle—fizzing and bubbling and overflowing until everything was covered in the sweet burning sensation of need.

She didn't say a word. Just held out a hand and beckoned him closer. Except she had a head start on him and he stripped out of his clothes as he strode toward her.

He put a knee on the bed and crawled over her—like a predator cornering prey.

"This is going to be like the first time," he growled as he lowered his body to hers.

A shudder ripped through him on contact. The warmth of her skin pressing against his sent sparks of pleasure to every inch of him.

She grinned up at him. "You'll have to remind me. Our first time was so long ago."

God. She was teasing him.

The return of confident Mel didn't simply get him in the balls; she got him in the heart.

He couldn't let her get away. And if he had to use their combustible sexual attraction to keep her, he would.

"Hard and fast." Grady gripped the sides of her head in his hands, held her still, and lowered his mouth to hers. "But first I'm going to kiss you like I mean it."

CHAPTER 31
TWO WEEKS LATER...

MEL WAS PUTTING the finishing touches on the homemade lasagna she was serving Grady for dinner.

In the last two weeks she'd cooked dinner most nights. Either at her place or his.

They'd gone back to living apart but hadn't spent a single day without sleeping in the same bed.

And the sex. Jesus. She'd thought the first time they'd slept together was hot. It had nothing on the firestorm that was their sex life now.

Her libido had returned with a vengeance once the morning sickness had subsided. It was like a switch had been thrown. One day she'd been nauseous from dawn 'til dusk, the next she wasn't.

The front door opened and she went to meet Grady. "Hey, you're early," she said as she headed toward him.

"Didn't shower." He smiled and pulled her in for a hug. "Thought I might be able to convince you to take one with me."

She couldn't resist his smile. All he had to do was aim it her way and her knees seemed to melt, her toes curled, and her insides tightened. "Hmm...let me put dinner in the oven and we'll have forty-five minutes."

He spun her around and pushed her in the direction of the kitchen. "Go. Meet you in there."

Glancing over her shoulder, she watched Grady's fine ass as he walked down the hall. It was definitely one of his best attributes. One she ogled whenever the opportunity arose.

Actually, she ogled all of him whenever she could. With a smile, she slipped dinner in the oven, set the timer, and went after her man.

She found him in the shower standing beneath the spray. Water bounced off his shoulders and back, ran down his legs.

Clothed, the man was hot. Unclothed...

Damn. Mel stripped and moved in behind him. "There is nothing more beautiful to look at than you in your birthday suit," she said.

"Oh yeah, there is." He grabbed her wrist, spun them both, and ended the motion with her pressed against the wall, his chest to hers. "You."

Before she could argue, he dropped his head and took her mouth with his.

The kiss was hot and wet and deep. Their tongues tangled, their lips clung.

She pushed to her toes to get closer, her fingers sliding over his slick shoulders in an attempt to bring him nearer.

They lined up all wrong when they were on their feet. Grady was so much taller than her; even when he bent his knees and she stood on her toes, things just didn't quite mesh.

She pulled her mouth from his and lowered her heels to the floor. And kept going.

He let her go, his eyelids going heavy as she sank to her knees.

"Mel."

She splayed her fingers and palmed his thighs, the hard muscles bunching at her touch. Leaning forward, she kept her eyes on his and swiped the length of his cock with the flat of her tongue.

"*Mel.*"

Her name was more growl than word and she took pleasure in seeing his eyes close completely.

They popped open again when she sucked the tip of him between her lips. His gaze burned into hers. His hands fisted at his sides.

She knew what came next. The second she pulled his shaft deep, those hands would grip her head, his fingertips pressing in as he fought to control the urge to thrust himself to the back of her throat.

She'd made it her mission to drive him out of his mind with her mouth. Turnabout was fair play after all, and Grady knew how to use his mouth on her in ways she'd never imagined.

They'd experimented with positions and toys and places but getting on her knees in front of him—sucking him dry— was her favorite, outside of having him thrusting into her pussy.

There was just something about this man pounding into her, the way he went deeper than anyone else, that had her screaming over the edge when he fucked her.

But for now she planned to give him the best blow job of his life.

Skimming her teeth down his length, she increased her suction, hollowing her cheeks, and swallowed around his head.

His hand sank into her hair, his fingers tangling in the wet strands, holding her in place as he flexed his hips.

Short, fast pumps rocked his cock over her tongue from throat to teeth, again and again. She relaxed her muscles, angled her neck to allow him deeper.

"Fuck. Mel." He let go of her head and planted both hands on the wall behind her.

Head hung low, he watched her suck him through hooded eyes.

"Take it," he growled. "All of it."

She gripped his ass and let him fuck her mouth. The carnal act of submitting to Grady never failed to dampen her pussy but tonight, with the thought of what she was going to tell him later—it threatened to take her over the edge without a touch.

"God. I'm going to…" He slid one hand over her hair and cupped her jaw. "Now's the time. If you don't want to."

The fact he never expected her to swallow always made her want to do it. She dug her fingers into his taut butt and sucked harder. It was all the answer he needed.

With a strangled groan, Grady sped up, driving his length into her mouth over and over.

He held the back of her head—not that she was going anywhere now—and with a grunt, pushed deep and came down her throat.

Mel swallowed and swallowed but couldn't take it all. He pulled out, his cock still pumping come, and dropped to his knees in front of her. "On your feet."

He gripped her waist and lifted her up. "*Grady*."

"Need to taste you."

Pushing her against the wall, he had her standing, legs spread and his face buried between them, before she took her next breath.

Sucking him off had gotten her so close it only took a few flicks of his tongue, a couple of thrusts of his fingers, and she was crying out in release.

She shuddered, her legs trembling as the orgasm slashed through her.

CHAPTER 32

GRADY PULLED Mel into his arms when he climbed to his feet. "Damn, woman. I think I'll wait to shower at home all the time."

She laughed. "We'll kill each other if you do."

She might be right. They were both struggling to breathe and he wasn't ashamed to admit his legs felt a little like jelly. "Let's get clean. Now that I've filled one appetite, there's another one making itself known."

"I made lasagna." She reached for the soap and he took it from her.

"Made?" He lathered his hands and passed the bar back to her.

"Yes..." she hissed as he ran his soapy hands over her breasts. They'd grown larger and more sensitive the further along her pregnancy went.

"God, I love your boobs."

"Make the most of them while you can. You'll have to share them soon."

"Share?" He cupped her, brushed the taut nipples with his thumbs. "With Little Bit?"

"Yeah."

"So you decided to breast feed?" They'd had the discussion during one of their many conversations about the changes her body was going through. She'd been undecided at the time. "Are you going to take time off work then?"

"Probably."

He wanted her to but he wouldn't force it. He'd offer his thoughts and let her make her own decisions. His stomach rumbled.

Mel laughed. "Hungry?"

Grady looked at the naked woman before him, his hands playing with her breasts, and thought his stomach wasn't the only thing feeling a little hunger. "For more than food."

She glanced down. "Wow. I don't think I'll ever get used to your recuperative power."

He grinned. "Like my sperm, it's super."

Laughing, she stepped away and rinsed off. "Dinner first. I've got something I want to talk to you about."

"Uh-oh. Did I leave my dirty socks on the floor again?"

"No." She smiled but it wobbled just a bit on one end. "I'll get dinner ready while you finish up."

She was gone before he could open his mouth.

Was it his imagination or had he seen uncertainty in her eyes?

The gnawing fear she might end things between them ate at him on a daily basis. He was always looking for the hidden meaning in what she said or did.

He closed his eyes and dropped his head back. He wouldn't get anywhere guessing. He had to man up and face whatever it was she wanted to talk about.

Grabbing the soap, he made quick work of washing away

the sweat from training. They'd trained hard in prep for tomorrow's away game against Tampa.

It was only a day trip but it was the first away game since his parents had left and while he had no doubt Mel would be fine, he didn't like leaving her.

Dried and dressed in a pair of sweats and a t-shirt, Grady entered the living room to see Mel had set the table. Normally they ate on the couch in front of the TV. "Special occasion?"

"I hope so," she said as she lowered a large pan to the table. "I also hope you're hungry. I made garlic bread too."

He watched her disappear back into the kitchen, a nervous skip in her step. Something was definitely up. Following, he asked, "Can I carry anything? Get drinks?"

"There's water on the table already." She held a basket of yummy-smelling breadsticks. "Unless you want something else."

He took the basket from her. "Nope. I'm good with that." Placing a hand on her lower back, he steered her to the table. "It all smells delicious."

She smiled and took a seat. "Let's eat before it goes cold."

"Mel."

"Not yet." She served him a huge slice of lasagna. "I'm sure you're starving."

Grady gripped her wrist. "It can wait. What's wrong?"

"Oh. Nothing." Lowering the food to his plate, she shrugged. "I'm a little nervous, that's all."

"Nervous? About us eating dinner?"

"No." She put her hands in her lap and took a deep breath. "Remember when we first found out I was pregnant?"

"Hard to forget." Six weeks, five days ago. Not that he was counting. Much.

"You said we should get married."

"You said no. Have you changed your mind?" *God, please, please let her have changed her mind.*

"No. Not about that."

"What then?"

"You asked me to do something else."

"Mel, whatever it is, just spit it out."

"I want to move in with you." The words rushed out of her mouth in one long sound. It took his brain a moment to work out what she'd said.

"Move in?"

She nodded.

He wanted to leap into the air and pump his fist but he had to be sure. "You mean pack up your stuff," he waved his hand around the room, "and move it into my house."

"Yes."

"No more splitting our time between the two places."

"No."

"Your driver's license will have *my* address on it."

She laughed. A happy, relieved laugh. "Yes. As in, I'll sell this place."

"Sell it?"

"I want you to know I'm serious about us. Selling it seems more permanent than keeping it and renting it out like a safety net."

Grady pushed to his feet. "We'll pack now."

"Sit down and eat. We can decide what furniture to keep and what to sell then we'll go to bed one last time here. Tomorrow while you're playing, I'll move my clothes and some light things to your place. There's no rush."

"Oh, there's definitely a rush. We're over six weeks late on this move."

CHAPTER 33

Placing the last garbage bag full of clothes on the backseat, Mel straightened and, pressing both hands to her lower back, stretched.

This was the final load for today. She'd overdone it but she would have all her essentials at Grady's house tonight. Everything else could wait.

Four trips back and forth from her house to Grady's had taken all day. He'd left before seven this morning and—she glanced at her phone—he'd be taking the field in about half an hour.

With any luck she'd be home in time to watch some of the game.

Home.

When had she started thinking of Grady's house as home?

Before or after she'd made the decision to move in with him?

It didn't matter. It wasn't really the house that was home. It was Grady.

Smiling, she headed back inside to make one final check and lock up.

She walked through the rooms and wondered why leaving wasn't hard.

She'd lived here since college. She'd saved every spare dollar—and some she couldn't—while in college until she had enough for a down payment.

She'd used her inheritance to pay off her student loans and open her business and when Shaw Events had taken off, she'd been able to pay the mortgage down fast.

Selling would bring a nice sum once the bank got its share.

She'd look at putting the money into a college fund. It was never too soon to start planning for her child's education. She ran a hand over her slightly rounded tummy.

In the last few days she'd noticed a bump forming. Grady had too.

Of course, he didn't curse the fact her pants were getting tight. He kissed and caressed the gentle curve and murmured sweet things to Little Bit.

Tears blurred her vision. She loved the way he'd nick-named the baby Little Bit. It was cute to see a six-foot-four wall of muscle go all soft and gushy over something that wasn't any bigger than a passion fruit right now. Not even as big as her fist.

There was no denying she was in love with Grady. If she hadn't been from the beginning, it hadn't taken her long to fall. He'd never once given her a reason to doubt his feelings.

He might not have said the words but he didn't have to. Everything he did told her the way he felt. She could wait for them both to be ready to say those three little words. For now she was getting in her car and driving home.

Home.

She sighed. She thought she'd known what home was.

She'd been so wrong. Before now, all she'd had was a house, four walls and a roof. Somewhere to keep her things and sleep at night.

With one last look at the place, Mel said goodbye to the past and got into her car.

Traffic was thick and chaotic. She took her time and tried to avoid those who thought the streets of Miami should be driven like a NASCAR track.

The highway wasn't any better. Her little sedan seemed to get hemmed in at every turn. Moving into the slow lane, she breathed easier as the huge SUV that had been riding her ass drove by.

"God. This is a nightmare." Her fingers ached where she gripped the wheel. The car in front braked and Mel did the same. They slowed further. "What the hell is going on?"

Leaning to the side, she tried to see between the cars but couldn't pinpoint a problem. Her phone beeped but she ignored it. There was no way she was taking her eyes off the road. Unlike the guy in the car beside her. He actually had his phone to his ear.

Traffic began moving again and she was soon doing the speed limit. Whatever had held them up was gone.

A flash of color drew her eyes to the rearview mirror. A red car was zigzagging through the lanes about ten cars back.

Shaking her head, she brought her gaze back to the traffic in front of her. Now that they were traveling at the speed limit, there was more space between vehicles.

The gaps allowed the red car to move through the traffic quickly and it was soon whizzing past her. The male driver had the window down, the radio blaring, and a cigarette in the hand he had dangling out the door.

"Idiot."

She'd barely uttered the word when he changed lanes at the exact moment a four-wheel drive did.

The two vehicles bumped off each other. It all happened so quickly after that.

The red car spun into a hatchback, the SUV into a minivan. The car behind the van clipped the rear quarter of the swerving SUV and shot off to the right, colliding with the sedan in front of Mel's.

She slammed her foot on the brake but it was too late.

Metal collided, glass shattered. Jolted from behind, her head snapped forward, slamming against the wheel. The world spun, flipped, thrashed back and forth. A piercing sound cut the air right before everything went dead silent.

Pain. So much pain. Everywhere.

She was lying on her side, the windshield no longer there. The glass beneath the side of her head cut into her cheek and her chest and stomach hurt where the seatbelt pinned her awkwardly. Blinking, she tried to focus except a haze of pink kept filling her eyes.

Noise returned. Shouts. Screeching brakes. More metal crunching. The car wobbled around her and feet appeared where the windshield used to be. How was that possible?

A man leaned in, gently touched her face. "Hey, are you all right?"

Mel tried to nod but nothing moved. She blinked twice and a groan gurgled in her throat.

"Okay. We're going to get you out." His face disappeared, denim covered legs in its place, and yelled. "This one! We need to get this one out before the gas goes up."

Her gaze lowered to the ground where scuffed workboots stood in a pool of liquid. And when she managed to take a breath, she smelled it.

Gasoline.

CHAPTER 34

GRADY LEFT the field with his teammates, winners again. They were having a brilliant start to the season. Today's game had been an easy win. Tampa may as well have stayed in their locker room with the way they'd played. Thirty-five to seven was not a good loss. Not that any loss was a good one.

The media converged on the sidelines and he found himself being waved over. Moving to the guy holding the mic, he smiled. "Hey."

"Grady, great game, considering. How'd you manage to keep your head in the game with what happened?"

What happened? He had no idea what the guy was talking about. "Like all games, I focus on the ball. The plays."

"Is there any word on how your girlfriend is?"

"My girlfriend?" What the hell did Mel have to do with this? Surely they weren't still interested in her being pregnant?

"The accident."

Grady's blood froze. "Accident?" His head snapped around to the bench and he saw Mark Mitchum and TJ Boldt coming towards him. Neither man had come with the team for today's game.

"The fatal highway pileup your girlfriend was involved in earlier today."

He ignored the reporter and strode toward Storm's President and Player Personnel VP. They met him halfway.

"What the fuck is going on?" Grady demanded.

"Walk." Mark grabbed his arm and directed them toward the tunnel. TJ moved in on his other side, taking his helmet. "Mel was in an accident. We've got a plane waiting—a car to take us to the airport. Your gear is already in the car."

Grady yanked his arm from Mark's and walked into the tunnel. "Is Mel all right?" The reporter had said fatal... No, he wasn't going there.

"Lexi is relaying status reports. Mel's car was one of fifteen involved in a pileup on I-95. She was trapped in the vehicle and they were unable to cut her free for nearly two hours due to the gasoline all over the road."

His knees buckled. "Oh God."

"Gotcha." TJ caught him around the waist before he hit the ground.

Grady grabbed the wall, bile rising in his throat. "Where is she now?" he managed to get out.

"On the way to the hospital, last time Lexi rang. She's on her way there too."

"C'mon, let's get in the car." Mark nodded to a guy who let them through a side door.

A black SUV was parked right in front and Grady climbed into the open back door. Mark took the front passenger seat and TJ slid in beside Grady.

"When did it happen?"

"Just before kickoff."

Grady spun to face TJ. "*Before kickoff?*"

"We didn't know about the accident or that Mel was involved until after you were on the field. I chartered a plane and TJ and I flew here to get you the second the game ended," Mark answered.

"You know Steve and his team have been keeping an eye on both of you since the media exposé a few weeks ago. One of their men heard the call on the scanner. Remembered her tag number and notified Hux who notified Steve. Then they called Mark," TJ explained.

"Does Lexi have any idea how bad she is? If she was trapped—"

"No." Mark turned farther in his seat to look at Grady head-on. "Lexi will let us know the second she hears anything."

Grady nodded. He watched Tampa pass by as the driver took them to the airport in minutes.

They boarded the private jet and Grady immediately strapped in, ready for takeoff.

As soon as they were allowed to move about, he went to the small bathroom in the rear of the plane. He stripped out of his uniform and raced through a shower before dressing and returning to the main cabin.

"Any news?" he asked as he buckled into the seat beside Mark.

He got a head shake in reply.

The next thirty minutes were the longest of Grady's life.

There was a car waiting for them when they landed and he recognized Steve, and the man with him could only be his brother.

Mark introduced him as Hux.

Grady shook his hand. "Does anyone have an update?"

"Lexi called as you were landing. Mel was conscious for most of the time she was trapped in her vehicle. She lost consciousness a few minutes before they pulled her free of the wreckage and they're checking for internal damage as well as head trauma."

"I need to get there." He moved toward the car and climbed in.

Steve took the wheel, with Hux up front, Mark and TJ flanking him in the back. Grady's phone rang as they pulled out of the airport.

"It's my mother. How the hell does she know?"

"It's all over the news. Which is why we've got ourselves a police escort."

Grady glanced up at Hux and saw the flashing lights of the cop car through the front window. Swallowing hard, he hit accept and pulled his phone to his ear. "Hi, Mom."

"Grady."

He closed his eyes against the wobble in her voice. "I don't know anything yet. I'm on my way to the hospital now. I'll call you back as soon as I know something."

"We're flying down there. Your father is booking now. Text me the name of the hospital so we can come straight there."

"There's no need—"

"Don't argue with me, Grady Archer Murdock. We're coming."

"Fine. I'll send you the info."

"Good." The line went dead.

"How much longer?" he asked.

"Five minutes."

He closed his eyes and leaned his head back.

She had to be okay.

Whatever happened, Mel had to be okay.

CHAPTER 35

GRADY HELD Mel's hand in his, forehead resting on top of them where he hunched over the side of her hospital bed. He'd been like that for hours. They'd wheeled her in, a bandage wrapped around her head, another on her left wrist, and a cast on her left ankle. She had numerous bruises, cuts, and abrasions, but luckily only the one broken bone and nothing life threatening.

Except she hadn't woken up yet.

The doctor assured him there was no swelling on her brain and she'd come around soon. He was finding it really hard to believe him.

All Grady wanted was to see her blue eyes without someone lifting her eyelids and shining a light in.

His mom and dad had been in and were somewhere in the hospital hunting up food and drink. Most of Storm management had shown up and his teammates had sent messages of well wishes.

His mother had dealt with most of it. Grady couldn't bear to leave Mel's side. If she didn't wake up soon...

"Grady?"

The hoarse whisper snapped his head up. "Mel? Baby?" He got to his feet and leaned over her. "God. I thought... I need to tell you something."

"I know."

"What?"

"The only thing I could think about while I was stuck in the car was I hadn't told you I love you."

For the second time today, Grady's knees buckled. He sank back into the chair. "I love you too. So much."

"Little Bit?"

"Fine." He squeezed her hand between both of his. "You're going to be fine." Reaching over he pressed the buzzer. "Mom and Dad are here. They flew down—"

"What? Why?"

He closed his eyes briefly. "You're all over the news. We both are."

"Really?"

"Yeah. It seems you being in a fatal accident and me getting flown home by private jet are equally as exciting and newsworthy as an unplanned pregnancy."

"Oh. Somebody died?"

"I don't know the details but Steve Goodman mentioned the police think the guy who started the incident is the only fatality."

"The red-car driver."

"You remember?"

"He was driving like a lunatic before he collided with a four-wheel drive. It was like dominos after that. Couldn't avoid it."

"Here." He was so relieved to see her awake he hadn't even thought to offer her a drink. Holding the straw to her lips, Grady waited until she drank her fill.

"Thanks."

"Good, you're awake." A nurse came into the room. "The doctor will be back in a few minutes. I'll just check you over while we're waiting."

Grady stepped out of the way but didn't go far. He wasn't going anywhere without Mel. Once the nurse had taken her temperature, blood pressure, checked her eyes, and asked how she was feeling, he moved back to Mel's side.

"When do you think she can go home?" he asked.

"The doctor will decide that but I'm thinking if she's good, tomorrow morning." She glanced at her watch. "That would be, later today."

"Ah, the patient is awake, I see." The doctor Grady had spoken to earlier entered the room. "How are you feeling, Ms. Shaw?"

"Sore."

"Yes, you will be for a while, I suspect." He took the chart the nurse held out. "Right. You have a broken ankle, a sprained wrist, a number of nasty bruises, and some cuts. The one on your head took twelve stitches but you'll be pleased to know the scan of your head didn't show any cranial damage."

"The baby?" Mel asked, her voice wobbling.

"Fine. Lots of protection around them."

Mel's eyes closed. "Thank—" Her eyelids shot open again. "Them!"

Grady grabbed her hand. "Easy."

Her gaze darted to his. "Them?"

The doctor chuckled. "I see we're going to do this again. Good thing you're already lying down. I won't have to catch you like I did Dad."

Grady smiled at Mel. "It wasn't exactly what I was expecting him to tell me about your condition."

"Wait. You're confusing me." She licked her lips. "Them as in more than one baby?"

"Yes. Twins."

"Oh God."

"Identical twins," the doctor added.

"*Two?*"

Grady laughed. "Yep. Double trouble for us."

"Okay, *one* I might have gone along with on my own, but two? Grady Archer Murdock, you will put a ring on my finger the second we leave this hospital! I will not be an unwed expectant mother of twins."

"Mel—"

"No. Seriously." She shook her head. "*Two!*"

"I'll get on that as soon as the doctor lets you out of here. But you'll have to come with me because I'm not leaving your side for the next ninety years." He leaned over and pressed his mouth to hers. "And, Mel, I need you to know I love you and want to marry you with or without our Little Bits."

CHAPTER 36

FOUR AND HALF MONTHS LATER...

"Don't you dare tell me it's too soon, Grady Archer Murdock! I'm thirty-six weeks, as big as a house, and my feet are swimming in a puddle." Pain gripped her abdomen, the contraction seemed to squeeze her from breasts to thighs, and more warm fluid ran down her legs. "It's fucking time!" she growled through gritted teeth.

"Okay. Okay. It's time."

The pain eased and Mel sucked in a deep breath. "Shit, that hurt."

"We'll get you some drugs when we get to the hospital," Grady said.

"I don't—" She doubled over. Well, as doubled as one got when you had two beach balls stretching your middle. "Argh."

"Breathe, baby. Like they showed us." Grady breathed the way they'd been instructed in the prenatal classes and Mel wanted to punch him in the face.

She grabbed onto the bed, her fingers curling into the bedding as another contraction took hold. "Fuck."

"Mel?" He stood behind her, held her by the hips as she slowly lowered to her knees. "We need to get you in the car."

"Not. Happening." She panted. "Call. Ambulance."

"What?" She could hear the panic in his voice and wanted to laugh, but another pain was building and the last one was barely over. "You can't have the babies here!"

Ignoring her yelling husband, she closed her eyes, rocked her hips from side to side and concentrated on breathing through the contraction. Fuck, it hurt.

"Mel?"

Her muscles relaxed and she slumped forward to rest her head on the mattress.

They weren't getting to the hospital.

Maybe later.

"Call an ambulance, then Dr. Nevins. Little Bit One is coming. Now!"

She sucked in a breath. Yep, LB1 was coming now. And LB1 was coming *fast*. Two more contractions and Mel was ready to push.

"Grady!"

"I'm here." He knelt beside her. "I've got Dr. Nevins on the phone."

"Put her on speaker." Mel panted in an attempt to slow down the arrival of LB1. "You're going to need those famous hands of yours to catch something other than a football."

"It'll be fine, Grady. Just do what I tell you," Dr. Nevins said.

Fine for *her* to say. How many babies had she delivered? Hundreds? Thousands?

And him? None!

"Grady?"

"Right here, Mel."

"I need to push."

"Go ahead with the next contraction, Melinda," Dr. Nevins voice came from the phone he'd switched to speaker and put on the bed beside them.

"Is she okay on her knees leaning on the side of the bed?" he asked.

"Whatever's comfortable for her. Just be sure to catch the baby before it hits the floor." The doctor chuckled.

Grady swallowed. Jesus. "Right. Catch the baby before it lands on its head," he muttered.

"Here it comes." Mel's back arched with the contraction.

"Get behind her, Grady. Make sure you've got your hands ready."

He crouched behind his wife and prayed he'd be able to make this catch.

The baby's head came into view and he was struck by the wonder of it. Mel was about to push into his hands the miracle they'd made together. "I see the head!"

"Okay, once the baby's head clears the birth canal, I need you to check the cord isn't wrapped around the neck," Dr. Nevins instructed. "I'm told the ambulance is two minutes out."

His baby's face came into view next and Grady quickly checked for the cord. "No cord."

"All right, Melinda. Next one. Grady, once the baby's head and shoulders are through, make sure to support the neck, and whatever you do, don't drop it. Things move fast from here."

The instructions weren't necessary. In the next second, Grady held a perfect little human in his hands. "Oh my God!"

"What? Grady, what's wrong?" the doctor yelled.

"Nothing. I'm holding a baby." He stared in awe. Big blue eyes blinked at him.

"What is it? Boy or girl?" Mel wanted to know before another pain struck her.

Grady looked between the baby's legs and smiled. "Boy. We've got a boy."

"And here comes his brother," Mel growled.

"What? I thought there was supposed to be a break between them?"

He reached for the blanket he'd dropped on the floor when Mel and Dr. Nevins convinced him this was happening here.

As quickly as he could, he wrapped his son and placed him a few feet to the left of where Mel knelt.

With a pained grunt, Mel arched her back and delivered their second son into Grady's waiting hands. He barely got a look at this one when the paramedics raced in.

"It looks like all the hard work is over," one of the men said.

The other laughed and said, "And Grade A once again proves not all his daring moves are on the field."

EPILOGUE
WINTER LAKE, NEW YORK

Fifteen years later...

"LOOK AT THEM GO," Sarah yelled, excitement dripping from each word. "It's like watching Grady all over again."

Mel smiled. Yeah, her boys weren't just the image of their father. They played football like him too.

It hadn't taken long to work out the Murdock twins were going to be football prodigies.

Grady had already fielded calls from scouting agents and the boys had barely finished their first year at Winter Lake High School.

From the minute they'd been born, Sean and Liam had been a team. They'd been her two little protectors from the minute they understood what it meant to take care of those you love. She would never get tired of the men in her life taking care of her.

Speaking of...

Grady headed toward her, Elle and Kate on either side of him.

Yeah, they'd gone into their second pregnancy expecting one and gotten another two.

The girls were four years younger than the boys and like the boys, Grady loved them to pieces. And spoiled them rotten. Hence why they now each held an ice cream when she'd said not until after the game.

Sighing, she turned back to the field in time to see Liam take a hit. She cringed. She'd never gotten used to seeing Grady get tackled and god help her, watching her little men take them wasn't any easier.

Not that they were little anymore. At fifteen, they were six-one and still growing.

"He's fine," Sarah said, her hand squeezing Mel's.

"I know, I know." She blew out a breath. "It's something I have to live with but I don't have to like it."

Sarah laughed. "Guess not."

Mel still didn't really understand the game. Grady had played for ten years before retiring and the boys had been playing since they could hold a ball and run, and yet the game was still mainly a mystery to her.

Not that she'd admit that to anyone. She might not be fully versed in the sport but she knew how to cheer and was enthusiastic in her support of the men in her family.

"Hey." Grady slid an arm around her waist. "I know you said—"

She held up a hand. "Don't waste your breath, big guy. They've got your number."

He shook his head. "Yeah, they do." He dropped a kiss on her forehead. "But then all the women in my life do."

Glancing past Grady, she asked, "Where's Max and Tate?"

"They talked Grandpa into a spin on the go karts."

"Oh god, they didn't?" Sarah exclaimed. Already moving

past Mel, she muttered, "I told him he's too old for that nonsense."

Grady laughed. "Grandpa is watching, Grandma, not riding"

"Well, thank god for that." She pressed a hand to her chest. "I about had a heart attack. I'll still go down there and make sure he doesn't get any bright ideas."

Mel smiled. "Those two are going to be trouble."

"What do you mean, going to be? They already are," Grady grumbled. "They're more boy than the boys ever were."

"For the boys, it's always been football. Our tomboys are all about speed." Mel laughed when Grady's face paled.

"We need more boys," he grumbled.

"Oh, no. We're not doing that again. I'm too old for that shit." Not to mention she'd carried six babies—two at time—in the last fifteen years. Three sets of identical twins were enough for anyone.

Although the last set had been a surprise. More so than the boys.

After Elle and Kate were born, they'd decided their family was complete and she'd had surgery to make sure of it.

Unfortunately—or fortunately in this case because she'd never wish away her babies—she'd chosen to have her tubes clipped and one of the clips had not 'clipped' well enough.

Six years after the surgery Mel had found herself knocked up again. Grady had been all about his super-sperm for years after that and while she loved her kids, she was done.

At forty-five her baby making shop was shut and never opening again.

"You know," Grady murmured as he pulled her close. "If you just let me love you, I bet I could change your mind." He nuzzled below her ear.

She melted into him and kept her mouth tightly zipped.

She wasn't fool enough to part her lips and say a word because if anyone in this world could change her mind it was Grady.

While their kids had his number, he totally had hers.

"I love you," he whispered into her ear. "And although I wouldn't object to more kids, I think the last two are going to break me."

Mel laughed. Their father wouldn't be the only male Maxine and Tatum broke in their lifetime.

At five they had everyone's number. She'd never met such smart kids and that was saying something because all their kids were smart.

But Max and Tate...yeah, they were going to break people and hearts.

"Enough about our hellions, talk to me more about this loving me you want to do." She grinned up at her husband.

"Well, if you let me love you for the rest of our lives, I'll make every one of your dreams come true."

Mel didn't have the heart to tell him he'd already accomplished that. Instead, she pushed up on her tiptoes and, pressing her mouth to his said, "If you let me love you for eternity, I promise the same."

"You loving me forever is my *only* dream, Mel."

If you enjoyed this book, please consider leaving a review. It only takes a few minutes and you'll be helping other readers find stories they'll enjoy, as well as supporting authors you love.

For what's coming next, latest releases, sales and more, join
Rhian's Royal Readers
http://www.rhiancahill.com/contact/newsletter/

ACKNOWLEDGMENTS

I know this one didn't really take place in Winter Lake but Grady is a hometown boy and after years in Miami playing football he was always going to bring his family home.

Fedora, Fedora, Fedora, what the hell are you going to do with me? I know, this time we didn't push that line too hard but we still nudged up against it. I swear (and yes, I've probably said this before but...) I'm getting the next one to you with time to spare. Thanks for keeping me inline and on time. Those days and weeks got all muddled up for a bit there.

I want to thank a couple of readers who never fail to make me smile. Shirley, Eileen, Amy, Kristy and Tamara, thank you for reading, thank you for the friendship, it's the latter I value most.

To every other reader THANK YOU THANK YOU THANK YOU. Without you I wouldn't be able to do what I love (most of the time and can't seem to not do even when I don't love it). Thanks for taking a chance on a couple who've been around a while. I hope you liked this fresh look at Mel and Grady.

xoxo

Rhian

ABOUT THE AUTHOR

Rhian Cahill is the alter ego of a former stay-at-home mother of four. With motherly duties rapidly dwindling, Rhian is able to make use of the fertile imagination she used to keep herself sane for all those years of slavery. Years spent living overseas and visiting tropical climates have helped inspire some steamy stories.

Multi-published in erotic romance, paranormal romance, and contemporary romance, Rhian, with the help of Mr. Muse, spends her days and nights writing.

When not glued to the keyboard you'll find her, book or knitting in hand, avoiding any and all housework as much as possible.

For more on Rhian –
Website – http://www.rhiancahill.com/
Newsletter signup – http://www.rhiancahill.com/contact/newsletter/
FaceBook – https://www.facebook.com/RhianCahillAuthor
Instagram – http://instagram.com/rhiancahill/
Twitter – https://twitter.com/RhianCahill
BookBub – https://www.bookbub.com/authors/rhian-cahill
Goodreads – https://www.goodreads.com/rhian_cahill

OTHER BOOKS IN THE WINTER LAKE SERIES

Love Me Like You Do

First comes love, then comes marriage, then comes baby…

wait, scratch that. Can we start with the babies?

Selling most of her possessions, breaking her lease and driving across the country in search of a man who might not want to see her probably wasn't such a great idea. Throw in an aging car with no heat, snow covered mountains and a rapidly expanding pregnant belly and Covington Valenti may have made the biggest mistake of her life.

When the woman who's had him twisted up for over a year turns up in Winter Lake Tristan Harding is more than happy to see her. What he's not so sure about is her extra baggage. But Tris is nothing if not a loyal friend and if Cov needs his help she has it—even if that means stepping up for someone else's kid.

Love The Way You Are

Who needs 20/20 vision to find true love?

There's something familiar about the gorgeous woman across the crowded club. When he "accidentally" bumps into her, Alex Dean is shocked to discover what it is. The tall, leggy blonde is none other than Sadie Emerson, his college math tutor—and the subject of more fantasies than he could count. Years later, she's looking better than ever. He has to have her. Tonight.

Does it really matter that she thinks she's going home with his buddy, Alec Dane?

Apparently it does because she sneaks away the morning after. *Twice.* First, when she discovers her mistake, then when she decides her upcoming move to Winter Lake makes them a two-day stand at best. But the sex is off-the-charts combustible, and Alex is already seeing stars, hearing bells...envisioning houses and picket fences and other things he'd never considered.

Now all he has to do is convince Sadie his feelings are real. His shy wallflower might consider him a mistake—but Alex has never been more certain.

When You Love Someone

When it comes to love the tough guys always go down the hardest.

Sophie Collins is used to the adoring attention from her fans but the overzealous one who cooked her a meal and left it—with heating instructions—in her fridge has gone too far. No longer safe in her own house, she hops a plane and travels halfway around the world.

He was sent to bring her home safe. But from the minute Sophie falls into Stone's arms he knows she's not the only thing in danger. He's a hardened warrior trained to kill with his bare hands and one too sweet too young pop singer is bringing him to his knees.

If he can't keep her safe and neutralize the threat he stands to lose more than his client. He'll lose his heart.

Wild Rush Of Love

Drinks aren't the only thing this barman is serving up.

Tending bar at Winter Lake Lodge, Rush Whelan enjoys all the fun with the female clientele, with none of the commitment. They come for vacation—and for Rush, in his bed—then they go. Until Sabreena. After spending her entire holiday together, Rush still can't get the shy beauty out of his mind. When he finds himself with some unexpected time off, there's only one thing to do—follow Reena home.

Waitress Sabreena Howe is grateful for the built-in family that comes with working at Pat's Pub. Mr. Collins and his brood have taken in more than a few strays, Reena among them. But even with their support, Reena has trouble letting people get close...including Rush. Despite their instant connection, Reena allowed fear to abort what could have been their amazing last night together.

When Rush shows up in Baltimore, Reena finally sets her trepidation aside, exploring her newfound sensuality even though she suspects another brief week together can only lead to heartbreak. Her home is here; Rush's is hundreds of miles away.

But the heart knows no time or distance. If Reena can redefine her definition of home, she'll find love is the greatest wild rush of all.

Hearts Are Wild Series

No More Talking (novella)

Dare You To (novella)

Mad Love

Boys Of Summer

Bondi Beach Boys

Sand, Surf And Sunnie

Only You Series

All Of You

Holiday Romances

Christmas Wishes

New Year's Kisses

Valentine's Dates

Secret Santa

Frosty's Snowmen Series

A Touch Of Frost

A Kiss From Kringle

A Taste For Kandy

Secret Confessions

Sydney Housewives – Virginia

Standalone Titles

Make You Burn